CIGAR CITY

Tales from a 1980s Creative Ghetto

PAUL WILBORN

For Bud Lee

I didn't move here to avoid chaos. I came for the excitement of it, and I was not disappointed.

Laurie Anderson

That world! These days it's all been erased and they've rolled it up like a scroll and put it away somewhere. Yes, I can touch it with my fingers. But where is it?

From Jesus' Son, by Denis Johnson

Cover photos: Bud Lee, with permission of the Lee Family
Inside photos: David Audet, by permission
Author's photo: David Audet, circa 1984

CONTENTS

ACKNOWLEDGMENTS

My thanks to David Audet and Bud Lee, my partners in Ybor all those years ago, who gave me more than I can ever repay. And to Bud's family - Peggy, Thomas, Steckley, Parker and Charlotte. Also, my Artists and Writers sister, Beverly Coe. Thanks to Jenny Carey and Mike Shea at Ybor Square and to Jill and the entire cast at La France. Thanks to all the artists, writers, actors and musicians who shared Ybor with me. To those brave Sicilians, Francesco and Francesca Capitano, along with Alice Carter, Boyd, Louise and Steven Wilborn and all the in-laws and outlaws in my vast Tampa family. For direct help with this project thanks go to Maxine Swann, Peter Meinke, Dorothy Smiljanich, Joe Hamilton, Jonah Hanowitz, Roy Peter Clark, Sergio Waksman, Richard Gonzmart, Maria Esparza, the Tuesday night writers table, and the coffee houses of St. Petersburg, where the bulk of these stories were written. And special thanks to Eugenie Bondurant for just about everything.

FOREWARD

I'm in my early 20s, my papers stamped with the seal of a state university, when Ybor City becomes the center of my world. I knew Tampa's old immigrant district as a child, but only as a historic relic. Eighty years earlier, my great-grandparents, Francesco and Francesca, met and married in Ybor, after crossing a restless ocean, clutching one-way tickets.

Their *Cigar City*, at the edge of the 19th and 20th centuries, is a polyglot place, cacophonous with the exclamations of wanderers from Spain, Cuba and Sicily, raising families on wages earned twisting Cuban tobacco into a luxury product sold as *La Rosa Espanola, Flor de Lovera, Tampa Girl.*

My *Cigar City* is a red-brick shell, hollowed by the great urban exodus and a post-war hunger for fast-burning, machine-made cigarettes.

Stepping into this void are artists, writers, actors, students - a new generation of American immigrants - fleeing a carbon copy suburbs in search of authenticity and cheap rent. Ybor isn't alone. In the late 1970s and early '80s, art ghettos bloom in many abandoned immigrant enclaves, like Manhattan's *Alphabet City*. Keith Haring and Jean-Michel Basquiat emerge from that quarter, while Ybor City lures James Rosenquist, Jim Dine, Chuck Close and other art world stars, who are drawn by the University of South Florida's Graphicstudio and a strong residential talent pool that includes the painter Theo Wujcik and the photographer Bud Lee.

In *Cigar City* we tread the hex block sidewalks in thrift store chic and howl like drunken wolves from the ledges of moon-soaked rooftops. Our second story apartments are spacious but squalid – best to shut your eyes in the rust-stained bathrooms. Downstairs a drugstore or tailor shop morphs into a vintage clothing boutique or pottery collective. Abandoned cigar factories are diced into artist studios and antique stores. Marble-pillared social clubs erupt in masked balls that beckon thousands of revelers. The club members, residing now in nursing homes or cemeteries, don't object.

Go on, *Cigar City* says, turn up the amps; stitch your fantasies into phantasmagorical costumes; launch parades led by hairy-chested "debutantes" or strutting roosters; hire a transvestite as the cover girl for your tabloid.

And while you are at it – go dig into the back of your closet and try your hidden passions and desires on for size.

Yes, there are brutal days when hummingbird-size cockroaches skitter past your head and forlorn box fans struggle to part steamy curtains of tropical air, but there are throbbing nights when we pogo to peg-panted guitarists or stage mock coronations that transform queens into kings. From a dozen gritty storefronts pots, paintings, poems and plays are served fresh daily – a buffet of creativity leavened by mugs of *café con leche*, tumblers of Spanish Rioja, and covert plastic baggies bursting with Columbian flowers.

The *Cigar City* in this story collection – which spans the 1980s - is both real and imagined. The stories and principal players are fiction. The buildings, backdrops and some of the supporting cast are real, though I do slide a few pieces around on the chessboard of time and space. I try to conjure friends I might have known, doing things my friends might have done, in a place I still can visit, but to which I can't return.

In the past tense of today, I realize my *Cigar City* was not so different from the place that greeted my great-grandparents. In *Cigar City* Francesco and Francesca found fertile earth where their youthful dreams could take root.

So did I.

QUARTER MOON

On full moon nights, Cilla would climb through a window onto the narrow rooftop between her apartment and the ledge over Seventh. She loved the metallic purr of the neon movie marquee that hung just below the wide ledge and the glow from it that bathed her in kaleidoscope colors - ruby, emerald and coral.

From there she could watch the moon emerge from a curtain of cloud to whitewash the wrought-iron balconies and red-brick battlements of Ybor City.

3

Under her huaraches, the roof was a crunchy cereal of coarse gravel and sun-bleached plastic beads, tossed by night-parade pirates as Cilla and her friends screamed and waved their arms. This ad-libbed terrace was why she loved her apartment – a place thousands of miles from the scrubbed, middle-class house where she had spent her childhood.

Her second floor apartment was accessible by a red door that opened onto Seventh, a few steps from the art-deco ticket booth of the Ritz – a 1930s movie palace, now peddling porn to suburban husbands, college students, and sailors arriving by taxi from the port nearby. Some nights Cilla was lulled into sleep by the moans of celluloid lovers.

There was no bell on the red door, so Cilla's visitors stood on Seventh, under the Ritz marquee, and tossed pennies that clattered against her windows.

Behind the red door were two flights of narrow stairs, carpeted long ago in red pile – now flat and faded to pink and stubbornly holding a faint aroma of rotting fruit.

In occasional calls to her family, the apartment morphed into a modern triplex near the university – not a smelly walk-up in an historic quarter that time had left behind.

She couldn't tell her mother about the rusty refrigerator or the hot plate and toaster oven on a splintered wood counter that passed for a kitchen. Or her closet of a bathroom - lit by two Virgin Mary candles from the Cuban bodega across the street. Cilla hung lacy pink curtains and thick white towels to distract attention from the rust stains scarring the tub and climbing up the galvanized pipe inside her toilet.

But her bedroom was wide and filled with light and the metal-frame bed she found tossed in an alley was buried beneath pastel pillows and a fuzzy white bedspread she had brought from Ohio. The tall west windows looked out over the jutting spires of downtown Tampa – a working class city always on the verge of metamorphosis, but

4

somehow unable to shed its own skin. The north windows of her living room revealed the rooftops and the sky above Ybor, once Tampa's immigrant quarter, now abandoned except for Cilla and a battalion of artists seeking urban authenticity and cheap rent.

She painted the walls pale blue, and Carl, a late-blooming abstract expressionist, and occasional guest in her bed, had added swaths of Florida clouds. Some mornings when Cilla awoke, the sky on the walls blended with the real thing outside the windows.

In another alley, Cilla had discovered a polished metal desk chair that fit through her window. Now the chair was her midnight perch - a glass of red wine on the ledge; a cigarette burning in one of the Buzz Man's ceramic Ybor ashtrays.

She took a long drag on a Benson and Hedges 100, and blew the smoke up toward the swollen moon. She flicked on a flashlight, the beam falling on two pages of formal cursive.

She wasn't sure what was holding her here as 1981 gave way to 1982 – now a full year after picking up her art history diploma from the University of South Florida. Maybe it was the gravel rooftop, the glow of the Ritz marquee or these handwritten words meant just for her – reasons as good as any to spend your 25th year living in a forgotten quarter of a port town like a refugee from a distant land.

***

General Avenal arrived for dinner every afternoon at exactly the same time. Cilla's shift started at three. The General marched in at four, as she was polishing glasses and wrapping stainless forks and knives in large paper napkins.

Rough Riders was a dark-wood pub inside an Ybor City cigar factory that now housed stalls for weekend antique vendors. A plank floor was set with bulky tables and heavy chairs that matched the food – thick burgers, finger-sized fried potatoes, Cuban sandwiches (ham, pork, cheese and pickles on crusty bread), and black beans and rice, sprinkled with raw onion. Tampa had been a staging ground for

Teddy Roosevelt and his soldiers before they charged the Spaniards
in Cuba. The name seemed to fit in this historic district – even
though the actual Rough Riders had camped across town.

The artists, postal workers and agents from the Customs office near
the port started circling the bar at five - happy hour got them two
beers for the price of one and deviled crabs for a dollar. So for one
hour, she and the General were usually alone.

She had his café con leche ready when he arrived. She set it down,
with some formality, in front of him.

"Priscilla, you look fresh and fetching today," the General said, in
English that was accented with the formality of his early life in the
Asturias region of Spain. ("We were never conquered, Priscilla.
Never!")

Cilla had slipped and told him her real name one afternoon. She
trimmed the first four letters when she moved to Ybor – along with
most of her almond-colored hair.

At the time, both decisions felt liberating and mature.

"Fetching" was never how Cilla had described herself – especially in
a waitress uniform – with her chunky Midwestern curves pushing
against the narrow black skirt and tight white blouse, her wide,
peasant feet tucked inside black Converse high tops.

The General however, was fetching. A fine-boned, meticulous man,
wrinkled but regal, barely cresting five feet, he always brought his
own starched white napkin, unfurling it with a wave, then smoothing
it out on his lap.

Today, as every day, his white pleated trousers were pressed, his rep
tie knotted at the neck of a blue dress shirt, and his navy blazer
adorned with military epaulets. His breast pocket was home to a
cluster of ribbons and medals. Snowfalls of dandruff, escapees from
his lacquered white hair, were the only aspect that wouldn't have
passed a military inspection.

Roddy, Cilla's neighbor and one of the art colony pioneers, swore the General was an old fraud – from the medals to his military title. The General had made a sketchy living selling military commissions and official government recognitions – suitable for framing - from various Central American fiefdoms.

But he had inherited the most beautiful building in Ybor – *El Pasaje* – a two-story fortress wrapped by a wide sidewalk encased in interlocking red brick arches. He lived alone upstairs, save for a grim-faced housekeeper who trudged bow-legged about Ybor – swathed in scarves, loose fitting black lace dresses and thick white cotton hose that wrapped her arched legs like bandages. The small oval of her face that emerged from the dark scarves was pale except for two scarlet circles of rouge on her cheeks. When she was out, she spoke - in Spanish - only to shopkeepers and returned to El Pasaje with grocery bags and the General's pressed uniforms from the laundry on 15th. In Ybor, they called her "The Widow."

To Cilla, this little man and his housekeeper carried inside them a large scoop of the magic dust that was Ybor City. They were a living link between the immigrant past, Italians, Spaniards, Cubans and Jews, eating, fighting, marrying, working, and dying here, and the painters, sculptors, and scene-makers who had inherited the place from them.

The fact that he was likely a con man made him that much more intriguing.

"You look especially Maya-like today," he said. "Did you know that?"

He liked to flirt with her this way – claiming she could have been the model for Goya's radical nude, *La Maya Desnuda*. The painting, confiscated during the Inquisition as obscene, captured not a traditional beauty, but a small-faced, full-bodied woman much like Cilla.

"I'm not feeling it today," she said. "But thank you."

"Did you read my paper?" he asked, carefully wiping his knife, fork and spoon with a pressed handkerchief pulled from his jacket pocket.

"I did," Cilla said, pulling a chair opposite him and sitting down.

"Then we are in agreement? No?"

"I will concede that Goya could go darker and deeper, but Velazquez is still the better painter. I'm sorry. He just is."

This was the standard argument between them. The General – a staunch Goya man –held the deaf Spanish painter above all the others – Picasso, Velazquez and most certainly Dali, whom the General referred to as "that damn moustache man."

Cilla loved Spanish artists – including Goya – and had written papers on most of them. But what she really loved was sparring with the General about art. He held his ground against her, unlike the young Ybor artists who knew little about art history and always deferred to Cilla's opinions, calling her "*La Profesora.*"

The General's paper – the two-page, hand-written screed she'd read on her balcony the night before - hadn't changed her mind. It was more rant than research. On matters of art – and most other subjects – the General's mind was made up and no amount of footnotes would change that.

But Cilla loved the arguments and his dinner table rituals: The polished silver placed carefully around the white China plate he brought from home. It reminded Cilla of the numbers on a clock. The coffee at 2. His round black glasses at 10.

Then, between them, circling the top of the plate like a tiara, the vials, pill bottles, satin pouches and eye-droppers containing his potions – milk thistle, cumin seed oil, bulky vitamin C tablets, pomegranate and blueberry extract, and his secret weapon, saw palmetto and stinging nettles gathered from the woods near Gibsonton and crushed with a mortar and pestle.

8

Life extension was the General's current passion and profession. He peddled his herbal wares via mail order and was his own best customer, though the frail little man didn't seem like an advertisement for his products. Cilla feared a strong wind could knock him over. His voice, however, was oaky and round.

He challenged her: "But have you seen a Goya with your own eyes? Not in a book or a slide? Have you?"

Cilla admitted she hadn't. The General looked around to make sure they were alone, then leaned across the table, his eyes locking on hers.

"I have one. No one knows this except me - and now you. And in this town of rogues and thieves, I beg you to keep my secret."

Cilla didn't blink.

"You have a Goya? Here in Ybor?"

The General nodded, then leaned back in his chair.

"Would you like to see it sometime?"

***

Cilla was instructed to arrive at 10 a.m. the next morning. The General had written her a note and urged her to be on time: "I believe in punctuality, Priscilla. It keeps the world turning on the proper axis."

At 9:59 she rapped on one of the double wood doors set along the passageway of *El Pasaje*. Cilla had "prettied up" for the meeting – deciding against her daytime Ybor uniform which was a Stanley Kowalski undershirt, faded jeans ripped at the knee (not a fashion choice but an actual rip from tripping on the jagged hex-block sidewalk coming back from work), and pink flip flops.

For the General, she chose a white cotton sundress, pinched a bit at the waist, with a scooped neck that showed off some cleavage. She had brushed what was left of her hair behind her ears and added a hint of peach lipstick, knowing the General would appreciate it.

After waiting for a long moment, she heard heavy footfalls on creaky stairs. Three bolts turned and one of the doors cracked open the few inches allowed by a rusted chain. The housekeeper scowled at Cilla. Her expression didn't change after Cilla introduced herself. She tried to hand her the invitation but the woman made no move to take it. So Cilla held it up where she could read it: *Please admit Miss Priscilla Kovach to my sitting room. Tuesday, March 21, 1982. 10 a.m.*

He had signed it with a flourish – *General Avenal.*

Without changing her expression, the old woman pushed the door closed and unhooked the chain. The untethered door swung open slightly. Cilla waited for the woman to open it wide, but when that didn't happen she pushed it open herself and saw the housekeeper's parentheses legs already waddling up the scuffed stairs.

The General, in his epauleted blazer adorned with ribbons and medals, stood atop the second-story landing, his arm outstretched in a formal wave, looking to Cilla like a military version of a ceramic lawn jockey.

He held that pose as she climbed the stairs. When she stepped onto the landing, he bent at the waist and swung his arm around toward the hallway, welcoming her in. From the hall, she passed through an arched doorway into a room that would have swallowed her apartment and the one next door as well.

Cilla had pictured the General in a formal sitting room, something from a Spanish court painting, but this wasn't it – though a pale blue tile floor did stare up at a pressed-tin ceiling almost 15 feet above. A slab of a couch and two heavy side chairs, wearing faded ruby brocade, were tossed randomly in a corner like ships that had run aground. Dozens of framed government proclamations – in primary colors and adorned with rippling flags and pressed official seals – hung from nicotine-yellow walls. Along one wall, towers of yellowed newspapers, books and magazines staircased across a mahogany dining table. A few steps away, a marble-topped credenza supported battalions of pill bottles, cloth bags, eye-droppers and clear glass jars.

Another table held a scale, a postage machine, stacks of large manila envelopes and coffee can bouquets of pens, pencils, scissors, rulers, feathers, markers and even a few tiny flags for countries Cilla couldn't identify.

Only one surface looked welcoming. In the center of the room, a table slightly wider than a piano bench held a crystal pitcher of orange juice, and two stemmed wine goblets. Straight-back carved oak chairs waited on either side.

"I am so pleased you could come," the General said, indicating one of the chairs.

Cilla sat.

The General sat opposite.

He poured juice into the glasses.

"The secret to my long life is in this glass," he said, raising it in a toast. "Vitamin C in juice form is the perfect supplement. But selling orange juice in Florida is like selling ice to Eskimos. So I have my other items" – he waved toward the cluttered table of jars and bottles – "and those I can sell at a nice profit."

"Do you have a goal?"

"For business?"

"For longevity," Cilla said. "I guess I'm asking how long are you planning to live?"

"That kind of goal. Oh, yes."

The General took another sip of his juice.

11

"In May of 1982, I shall celebrate 85 years on this planet. So I have touched the 19th century and spanned the 20th. My plan is to see the 21st arrive. It is just 18 years away and December 31, 1999 shall be a night worth celebrating."

"How about we meet here that night and celebrate together?" Cilla said, flirtatiously, enjoying the idea of a distant date with him.

"Not here, please," said the General. "Someplace important and alive. Buenos Aires is perfect in December."

"OK. Buenos Aires it is. I'll file for my passport now."

She clicked his glass in agreement. He took a long drink, then set the glass down. He reached across the table and Cilla felt sandpaper fingers brush her wrist.

"I've never asked … why are you here?" His gray eyes, behind the black frames, locked on hers.

"You invited me..." Cilla hesitated. "Oh, you mean here, in Ybor?"

"This building tethers me like an anchor, but you are free - and young. Ybor is a corpse in a red-brick coffin. You should be somewhere that's alive."

"I guess I'm drawn by death and decay," she joked, grasping for the real answer. The one she had been asking herself. "Really…my friends…I mean, lots of talented people live here, probably the only interesting people in this city. Painters, writers, sculptors. I don't know – it's… fun?"

The General shook his head, and his fingers slipped from her wrist, seemingly disappointed with her answer.

"Fun? Fun is overrated. It can be a trap. Frankly, I don't see any future Goyas, or even Picassos here. Mostly just a bunch of moustache men, being provocative for the sake of it. That's not art."

"Again, we disagree…" Cilla said, suddenly feeling a bit hurt. But then she realized they were simply jousting again. She smiled at him. "And someone told me they had some real art to show me. Right?"

The General stood. He leaned in so close she could feel his breath on her ear.

"Follow me," he whispered.

***

Carl got to the bar late that night, still in his paint-smeared T-shirt and jeans. Unlike some of the artists in Ybor who never missed a happy hour, Carl worked long hours at his easel, stopping only when his stomach was too empty or he had to work an odd job to help pay his rent.

He was 26, with an MFA in painting from NYU, but he looked like a lost teenager – long-necked and gangly, with dense curled spires of hair that reminded Cilla of Art Garfunkel.

She wasn't sure if he was shy, introverted or just odd. She had worked hard to get his attention when they first met and now, if she reminded him and he wasn't deep in a new painting, he almost passed for a boyfriend.

He didn't call. He didn't take her out. But he kept a toothbrush at her apartment. And sometimes he tossed pennies at her window from the sidewalk below. She'd climb out and look over the ledge, find him down there, looking uneasy, offering a nervous smile up in her direction.

That night, Cilla brushed his hand as she delivered a mug of beer. She touched his shoulder when she set down the burger a bit later. He apparently was paying attention. When she dropped off his check, Carl actually reached out and took her hand – holding it for at least 10 seconds.

Later, as he snored quietly beside her, Cilla breathed him in – moving past sweat, beer, a hint of oil paint and mineral spirits to find his real aroma, a mix of cedar and pine that Cilla loved.

She had been hungry for him since her visit with the General earlier in the day.

She rolled away, escaping as quietly as she could from the squeaky bed, pulling a silk robe around her. She grabbed cigarettes and a lighter, and slipped out the window.

Why had the meeting with the General excited her so? That old relic from the past was not someone she pictured in any erotic fantasies.

But she had felt a tingle as he led her into his bedroom to see the Goya.

Even at 10 a.m., the room felt like daybreak – thin sheets of light seeped in from the edges of thick curtains that covered two floor-to-ceiling windows. The General made no move to turn on a lamp.

In the half-light, she could make out the ornate carving of his bed frame and two oil portraits that might be the General as a younger man. The General knelt in a shadowy corner. He switched on a flashlight that revealed a black floor safe, with gilded edges, a chrome handle and a combination knob. Three turns – right, left, then right – and he pushed the silver handle.

The safe opened.

The focused beam of the flashlight revealed papers and files. The General pushed them to one side and, like a man handling explosives, he gingerly pulled out a small framed painting no more than 12 inches high.

"Come," he said, moving toward the tall window, pulling back one side of the heavy curtains and holding the frame up to the morning light.

Cilla caught her breath.

It was a miniature version of Goya's famous nude, looking up coquettishly from an emerald green fainting couch, her head and back resting on white pillows and a silk throw.

The General, seemingly afraid to speak too loudly while holding his miniature masterpiece, whispered in Cilla's ear.

"The model for the Maya was Pepita Tudó, mistress of Goya's patron, Manuel de Godoy. When it was seized by the Catholic bastards and Godoy was disgraced, Goya secretly painted this miniature for him. Something Godoy could keep with him during his exile. I first saw it in Argentina after the war."

Cilla was sure the painting was a fake – Goya's life and all his work was very well documented. The General's story didn't seem plausible, but this miniature was clearly very old and the work of a talented artist.

"How did you…?"

"Best not to ask. It took five years of negotiating but it is mine, or at least I am the caretaker of it for now. Age steals so many things you think you can't live without. In the end, all you have left is art."

Shouts from the street below – two sailors leaving the Ritz, arguing in some Slavic tongue – snapped Cilla back from the General's room to her Ybor ledge. She took a long drag on her cigarette and looked up, searching for even a sliver of a moon. But a wave of fog– cast pale pink by the smoldering vapor streetlights along Seventh – had washed in from the bay, blotting out the sky.

She wished she hadn't laughed. It was nerves probably. Or the thought that the General was so sure this tiny forgery was the real thing. Whatever the reason, at the moment the General handed her the painting, a small snort of laughter had escaped.

Cilla apologized, but the General took the painting back, locked it in the safe and, without a word, turned and ushered her to the front door – saying only a quick goodbye as she walked down the stairs.

She turned back when she reached the front doors, hoping to tell him again that she was sorry, but he was gone.

***

That afternoon the General did not come for dinner. Cilla was sure she had hurt him and he was punishing her.

The next afternoon at 3, as she wrapped silverware in paper napkins, the old housekeeper swept into Rough Riders, her white hair uncombed and uncovered.

"El Generale! El Generale! Senorita, por favor…" she was begging Cilla and tugging at her arm, tears edging down the tiny creases in her painted face.

Jenny, her manager, looked over from the bar. "Go," she mouthed to Cilla.

El Pasaje was across a courtyard and a wide brick street from Rough Riders. Cilla ran, leaving the old woman huffing and stumbling behind her. The double doors to Avenal's lair were thrown open.

Cilla raced up the stairs.

The General, wearing his dinner uniform, was sprawled on the landing, his head pressed to the floor, white tablets and tufts of herbs littered around him.

Cilla had to bend down to see his eyes – wide open and ticking left and right. Half of his mouth was pressed shut. Thick, milky saliva seeped down his chin and pooled on the floor. She rolled the old man over onto his back. She looked deep into his eyes and spoke his name.

The General's right arm came up in three spasmodic jerks: his eyes searching; his tiny fingers clutching vainly at the sleeve of her blouse.

***

The red and white ambulance that brought the General home from *Centro Asturiano Hospital* to *El Pasaje* four days later was a long, low-slung station wagon, rear fins rising like chrome wings with a single cherry red light on the roof.

Cilla watched from the sidewalk as two, white-coated men carried the General through the double doors and up the stairs – cargo so light each man needed only one hand on the stretcher.

Cilla had tried to visit the General at the hospital, itself a decaying leftover from Ybor's glory days, but had been turned away.

"No visitors. Family orders," said a tired-looking woman at the reception desk, her finger pressed against an entry in a leather-bound logbook.

The day after the General returned home, Cilla knocked on the double doors.

When the Widow appeared Cilla could see she had been crying. She took Cilla's arm and they climbed the stairs together.

In the General's bedroom, a brass floor lamp threw a circle of gold light over the tiny figure sunken into the sheets.

To Cilla, the General seemed more vapor than flesh and blood. His white hair tousled. His skin paper-thin and dry, with narrow veins running below that reminded Cilla of the garden snakes that hid in her backyard in Ohio.

Turning away to fight back tears, Cilla saw the safe in the corner. The door was open, the papers and the painting were gone.

Cilla leaned close and whispered the old man's name, her hand pressed against his cheek. The General's eyelids flicked open. One side of his mouth was pinched shut, but the other side quivered as if he were struggling to speak. A moment later, she thought she heard him exhale a single word: "Nothing…"

For the next hour, Cilla sat at his bedside, reciting everything she could remember about Goya and Velazquez, her voice steady and, she hoped, comforting. While she spoke, she held his right hand, feeling his sandpaper fingers clutching hers.

She came back the next morning, bringing Carl - who spoke passable Spanish - to talk with the old woman.

"They brought him home from the hospital to die in his own bed," she explained. The General refused to eat or drink anything save a few drops of water.

"Ask her what happened to his painting," Cilla told Carl.

Two days after the stroke, a nephew – using his own set of keys - had come into the building, the old woman told them. He had rummaged through the General's papers and emptied the safe.

"I could not stop him…"

She offered them tea, then left to make it.

Carl kissed Cilla on the forehead, then pulled a chair to the bedside. Cilla sat, taking the General's hand, and felt his fingers clinching around hers. She turned, pressing her face into Carl's stomach, letting tears fall.

"I have to do something," she said, looking up at Carl. "Will you help me?"

***

When Cilla tied back the curtains by the General's bed, the glow from the full moon bathed the room with a gauzy luster.

The Widow had closed her bedroom door an hour earlier, grateful for Cilla's offer to sit with the General overnight. When Cilla heard the penny clink against the window, she slipped down the front stairs and unlocked the double-doors.

Seeing Carl there in the moonlight holding her red suitcase, Cilla felt a sudden itch of anticipation, like a bride packing her lingerie for the honeymoon.

"All good?" Carl asked.

"All good," Cilla replied, letting Carl slip past her and locking the door behind him.

The preparations took almost an hour.

When all was ready, Carl wiped the General's face with a wet cloth, and whispered his name. In the moonlight, the old man looked boyish, unwrinkled. Slowly, his eyelids rose, like the gentle lifting of a roll-top desk. Carl eased the old man into a sitting position, and snuggled into him, holding him upright with his own body. He carefully balanced a pair of glasses on the General's face.

Behind the dark frames, the General's eyes blinked as he took in the room. The old brocade couch had been pushed into place a few feet from his bed and when he saw it, the side of his mouth that could move began to quiver. His left arm edged up, a single stalk of a finger uncoiling from a clenched fist.

There on the couch, bathed in moonlight and reclining atop two white pillows and a silk throw, was *La Maya Desnuda*: arms raised, hands open behind her head; ringlets of curls falling to one shoulder; breasts firm and round; a tuft of almond-colored hair where her legs came together; and a sly, coquettish smile on her peach-colored lips.

SMOKE

I'm stuffing the last lid into my old blue backpack when I see Barry outside my window – a fleeting figure in the flat metallic light that passes for a winter sunset in Ybor.

I yank open the front door thinking I'll surprise him but he's already there on my sagging porch, wearing shorts in January, with that paintbrush hair falling across his forehead and down over one eye. A black Bad Taste in Outer Space T-shirt stretched tight across his beer and burger waistline.

"Buzz, you gotta hear this," he says striding in.

He flips me an album cover with one hand. He carries the shiny disc aloft with the other, his pinky through the center hole like a waiter balancing a tray.

"Prep the bong while I put it on."

Perhaps we've been neighbors for too long. Not just here on 4th Avenue for the past year, but Barry also has the stall next to me at *El Sama*, the abandoned cigar factory turned arts studio two blocks away. We both toss clay. Barry manages to make money doing it. I need my night job to keep me afloat.

Barry assumes I'm always ready to get him stoned when he arrives like this. I'm usually happy to oblige, but tonight is a work night and I'm trying to keep my wits about me. Truth is, I have trouble counting money when I'm lit.

"Listen, I gotta make some stops tonight. It's Thursday," I tell him, knowing this won't make any difference.

"And you're starting your Thursday night listening to *The Swimming Pool Qs*. Out of Atlanta, but the guy grew up in Lakeland. They're playing the next Artists and Writers Ball."

"Barry…"

"Two songs. Okay, one song." He drops the needle on a hard-hammering Southern Gothic number called Stock Car Sin.

Barry flops down on my couch and pulls the silver tray towards him. I guess when your coffee table is home to a purple bong and a finely ground mound of herb on a silver dish, people assume you're always ready to light up.

Flame leaps from my brass Zippo, the bong bubbles, and next thing I know four or five songs have played and Barry and I are doing a furious pogo around the living room to a thrasher called *The A-Bomb Woke Me UP!*

One landing puts me directly in front of my window and there's
Barry outside again – except it can't be Barry because he's just
collapsed back onto my couch.

"Did you see that?" I yell toward him over the thrumming speakers.

"What?" he hollers back.

"Somebody's outside the window!"

I spring even closer to the window. The glass is cloudy from being 70
years old and from me not having ever bought a bottle of Windex.
But I can see well enough to know there is nobody outside, just the
peeling paint of Barry's matching shotgun shack and his identical
window five feet away.

The song finishes and I move over and lift the needle.

"I swear there was somebody out there."

"And then…" he says, as he stuffs more green powder into the silver
pipe head, "…when you look out the window a few seconds later,
nobody's there. Right?"

I nod, the sudden absence of music making the room feel like it's
throbbing. I sit down next to Barry and rub my eyes, causing a freight
train loaded with hieroglyphics to crash, spilling the whirling patterns
all over the inside of my eyelids.

"It's the 'litos," Barry says. "They're out there, man. I've seen 'em in
my windows, too. Like a flash, then gone. Fuckin' 'litos. I heard
Jenny got mugged after she closed Roughs the other night. A 'lito
with tattoos all over his neck pulled a knife."

Barry's voice seems to be coming through a string stuck in a tin-can
telephone. I open my eyes and the room settles down. Smoke
streams from Barry's lips.

"What are you talking about?" I ask.

"Marielitos! Where you been? Castro's killers and crazies! He put 'em on the boats and shipped 'em here. Now we got a fuckin' crime wave. You best watch your back, Buzz Man."

***

OK, it's no secret in Ybor that I'm The Buzz Man.

I was born Robert Krane – with a K – but all my life I've gone by Buzz, based on the fact that my dad, Major Robert Krane, USAF retired, gave me a buzz cut with his Norelco every Saturday.

My brother too.

And by buzz cut, I mean down to scalp level, flattened out on top, with just an inch left in the front that you greased with Butch Wax so it stood straight up like a follicle fence.

My junior high classmates who were growing Beatles mop tops would make buzzing sounds when I came to school. But truthfully, I liked "Buzz."

And now that I'm living in the Quarter with hair that falls in a Rod Stewart shag to my shoulders, the nickname has morphed into my brand.

The coffee mugs, ashtrays and pitchers I make at *El Sama* with "YBOR" on the handles - look underneath and there it is: "BUZZ MAN."

And in my night job – keeping the arts colony *herbicized* - it's the perfect handle.

"Hey, Buzz Man, good to see ya! What you got for me today?"

Anyway, I finally break away from Barry and my bong, both lit, and head out to make my sales calls - a door-to-door peddler in faded jeans and a torn sweatshirt.

Lacking actual weapons, I arm myself against killer refugees with fingernail clippers, ready to slide out the sharp nail file in case of trouble. Since I don't own a flashlight, I pocket the brass Zippo, leaving Barry to find his own flame.

***

Frankie and Josh are my first stop, two blocks away on Fifth in a cluster of well-kept craftsman bungalows that survived Ybor's decline in the 1960s and '70s.

The south edge of the old Latin Quarter where I live is dark. The streetlights are standing but most bulbs are broken or burned out. Walking casually – so as not to draw attention - seems like the best idea. But with each footfall, I sense someone's breath on my neck. When I spin to confront them, nail file ready, the sidewalk is empty.

A car screeches around the corner in my direction and I decide to sprint the last two blocks to Josh and Frankie's, bounding up concrete steps onto their porch. I knock hard, my head swiveling over my shoulders, eyes darting left and right.

Lights are on inside, but no one answers.

I pound again.

Framed in the yellow porch light glow, I turn to face the street, my heart hammering.

Finally, a dead-bolt thunks.

"Buzz Man, you're late. We were getting worried about you," Frankie says, pulling open the carved wooden front door. He's naked except for a thick white towel around his midsection, his wet hair dripping onto the polished wood floor.

"You see anybody following me?" I ask, slipping inside.

"This is Ybor," says Frankie, stepping onto the porch and giving the block a quick scan. "There's nobody out here after dark. You need to cut back on the herb, my friend. It's the root of most low-level paranoia."

"It's not the herb," I tell him as I step through the open door. "It's the Marielitos. Castro's killers and thieves. They're lurking outside my place."

"You talking about the refugees? We've had some stuff disappear off the porch," Frankie says. "Flip-flops, an old bird cage. But I hadn't thought much about it. "

"Barry told me Jenny got robbed and cut as she left Roughs the other night. Guy had tattoos all over his neck."

"You sure? I saw her yesterday. She seemed fine. "

"They're out there and we all need to watch out," I tell him.

Standing still releases more swirling hieroglyphics. This time I see them with my eyes open. The dark forms shut down my vision. I take a deep breath, sucking in the mournful minor-key melodies floating through the house.

"Forget the Marielitos, watch out for the residents," I hear Frankie say, a little louder than necessary. "Josh is in a mood."

"I am not in a mood," Josh yells from somewhere in the house.

"He's playing Chopin and when Josh plays Chopin, he's in a mood," Frankie says. "We're in the tub room. Come on back."

Frankie pads away, leaving me to regain my bearings. When the world comes back into focus, I'm in a high-ceilinged living room stylish with antique side tables, deep white couches, and leather club chairs - all topped with Frankie's grandmother's hand-made lace doilies. Five of Josh's stained glass table lamps – jutting geometrics the size of toasters – glow from side tables and on the mantle over the fireplace.

Hanging above the mantle is Bud Lee's *American Gothic* portrait of Frankie and Josh.

Bud, a photographer who shoots for *Esquire* and *Life*, is Big Daddy of the Ybor arts scene and loves recreating classic paintings with a kinky twist. In this one, Frankie holds the pitchfork, wearing faded overalls and nothing else, looking like a muscled Sicilian Adonis: jet-black curls; a nose that belongs on a Roman coin; and lips set in an Elvis-like sneer. Josh – a full-foot shorter than Frankie with the body of a teenage boy - plays the woman: shoulder-length, sand-colored hair pulled back into a bun; his nipples showing just above the white bric-a-brac of an apron; his fine-boned face constricted like he's just swallowed a lemon.

The thud of a pump kicking on brings me around and I head back to the tub room.

Frankie inherited this house from his grandparents, who moved to Ybor 80 years ago from Santo Stefano, a tiny village in the southern hills of Sicily. When Josh wanted a hot tub, Frankie sank one into the wood floor of a back bedroom, replaced the walls with glass and surrounded it with an outdoor garden of bamboo and orchids.

I find Josh and Frankie there, up to their armpits in the bubbling tub, steam rising like cigar smoke toward an exhaust fan in the ceiling. The garden outside is lit from below, making the windows disappear, so the room feels like some kind of magic oasis.

There are four twenty-dollar bills on a small metal table in the corner. I pick them up and replace them with two fat bags of buds.

"I'm having tea tonight, Buzz. You want some?" Josh says, lifting one of my electric blue YBOR mugs from the ledge of the tub. Two more of my mugs share the ledge with one of Barry's big raku teapots.

I blame the bong hits with Barry. At that moment, I completely blank on the fact that the tea Josh drinks in the daytime is different than the tea he sometimes serves at night. And at the moment, my mouth feels like I swallowed a wool sock.

"Sure," I tell him.

Josh pours. I take a long sip. The tea is thicker than I expected, and flavored with honey. I swallow the rest in one gulp.

"Chamomile?" I ask.

"Mushroom," Josh says, smiling now. "That's the kind of mood I'm in. Enjoy."

I'm thinking a mug of mushroom tea is probably not the best idea tonight, but since I've had one, another couldn't hurt. I hold out the mug and Josh pours. As I down the second cup, I notice the mournful piano notes have followed me into the tub room.

"So this is Chopin?" I ask.

"Arthur Rubinstein doing the Sonata No. 2 in B flat minor. Chopin at his most funereal. He actually had a skeleton set up in his apartment in Paris to inspire him while he composed it. You hear life and death playing out their eternal battle – and, of course, death wins. It's the essence of Romanticism."

That's Josh: ask a simple question, get a graduate-level lecture. Josh is an oboe player and Julliard dropout who gave up classical music for stained glass. Frankie, who works construction, prefers Springsteen to Chopin.

"Josh calls this romantic," Frankie says, splashing water onto his partner's face. "When I want romantic, I play Barry White. Buzz Man, you want some of this tub?"

I shake my head.

"Miles to go before I sleep, but thanks."

27

"Buzz," says Josh, raising a thin, dripping arm and taking my hand, his 'schroom'd pupils – translucent circles the size of dimes – holding my eyes. "I'm feeling darkness passing over the Quarter tonight. Move toward the light and keep your wits about you."

***

Back on the street, despite Josh's warning and Chopin's mournful melodies, I'm strangely giddy, like a kid waiting for the bell to ring on the last day of elementary school. My nose is full of the nutty flavor of roasting coffee from the Naviera mill a few blocks away. There's a hint of a chill in the air. The streetlights leading from Fifth to Seventh – Ybor's main drag – pour golden puddles of light onto the wide sidewalk. The whole scene has a Technicolor glow.

I start humming "We're Off To See The Lizard" and suddenly I'm a loose-limbed scarecrow skipping through the circles of light. My wits are definitely about me.

Then I run into the police car.

The exact details of how my hands slapped the hood of the cruiser are not clear. One minute I'm skipping and singing and the next the chase lights are flashing red and blue, the cop's window is whooshing down and I hear an angry voice from inside yelling, "Hey! Hold it right there!"

The weight of a backpack full of fat Jamaican buds suddenly seems like an anvil pulling me underwater.

But I have my wits about me and I hear their message echoing off the bones inside my head: Run!

So I do.

Sprinting through the yard of an abandoned casita, then into the alley behind Seventh Avenue, headed anywhere that's not the back of a police cruiser. My legs seem to be operating completely out of my control. I'm floating above, taking in the scene: a lone figure with a backpack scampers through a dark alley; red and blue lights spin atop a white cruiser that screeches into the same alley; a chrome bumper bangs into galvanized garbage cans, their silver lids roll away like lost shields.

The rusted rungs of a fire escape appear just ahead. I see myself grab the bottom rung and in some superhuman feat of strength, yank myself up so I can grab the next one. My feet find support and I scamper up. I'm screaming – "Yes" – just as two hot wires surge through my lower back.

Fuck man. They shot me!

An open window appears and suddenly I'm inside, face down on the wood floor, a roiling sea of black hieroglyphics pulling me down, down, down.

***

"Hey, Buzz Man, you OK?"

Heaven, at first glimpse, is a serene, candle-lit place. A female angel, wearing white, leans over me, her velvet hand resting on my forehead.

"Now, take a good breath," the angel says. So I do. My lungs fill with pink and purple cotton candy and I exhale tiny crimson butterflies.

"He's coming around," I hear the angel say. I blink a few times – the angel smiling down at me looks a lot like Kathy, who lives in a cluster of apartments above Seventh called "Upstairs South."

Now, a male angel hovers over me who sounds a lot like Roddy, Kathy's neighbor and one of the customers on my route.

"Buzz Man, you had us freaked," I hear the male angel say. "We thought you were one of those Marielitos trying to rob the place."

"I'm not dead?" I hear myself asking.

"Kathy had the frying pan in her hand, but we recognized the blue backpack so we let you live," the male angel says.

Not being dead seems like a good thing now. And somewhere down in the gauzy prism of my brain, I feel my wits trying to knit themselves back together. A few blinks and the room comes into focus - at least the part I can see from flat on my back.

There are the pressed tin tiles of the ceiling. There are the tips of my tennis shoes. Lowering my chin, I notice my legs are raised, knees bent, and my Converse All-Stars are resting in thick metal stirrups that rise from a table that supports the rest of me.

"Where?" I manage to ask.

"You came down in Dr. Leto's office, so we put you on the exam table," Roddy says.

"And I thought you'd enjoy the stirrups. Men never get a chance to try those," Kathy says.

Dr. Leto was Ybor's last physician, a gynecologist who, Roddy swears, performed abortions after hours. Still practicing at 90, the old doctor was found dead in his office chair a few months after Roddy rented the apartment next door. Dr. Leto left an office full of antique equipment - metal examining tables set on arched legs, rusting medicine cabinets, and dozens of silver-plated pincers and probes right out of some B-movie torture chamber.

Two years later, it all sits just as he left it. No family ever came to claim anything.

Roddy waves and heads back down the hall, leaving me alone with Kathy.

"Try to sit up, Buzz Man," she says, her hands behind my shoulders, lifting me up.

Kathy, I should mention here, is my Ybor Dream Girl - an occasional actress and drama student at the community college, with close-cropped blond hair, pillow lips and a bony boy body that comes with swimsuit-model boobs. I realize her angel outfit is actually a white, terry cloth robe. And I also realize this is the closest I've ever been to her despite many clumsy attempts to snag an invite into her life or at least her bedroom.

I smile as she lifts me, until the electric prods ignite in my lower back sending sparks down my legs.

"Ohhhh. I think I'm shot. The cops…"

"I think maybe you pinged your back falling through the window," Kathy says, lowering me down. "What were you doing on the fire escape anyway? That thing is barely attached to the wall anymore."

She's close to me now. Her lips. Her teeth. Her breath cool on my face. I feel my wits scattering again. I know I should tell her something.

"I love you," I hear myself saying.

"Really? Tell me more," Kathy whispers, her hand soft and warm on my forehead.

"Sometimes I see you at a party or Rocky's auction and for a minute or two I just stop breathing," I say.

This simple revelation shocks me. I'm a severe incompetent when it comes to girls – not the sex part, the talking to them part. But something – the tea, the chase, maybe the Chopin – has lubed my tongue. These words just ease out.

"I didn't know," she says. "That's very sweet. What was that first part again?"

"I love you?"

Kathy slides her hand from my forehead, letting her fingers brush down my cheek. She leans in and her lips touch mine, leaving a scent of lavender and patchouli. A sudden thickening between my legs lets me know I'm going to live.

"You rest here a while. I've got to get back to work," she says. "Come to Roddy's when you're feeling better."

It feels good where I am, my feet in the stirrups, my head on a tiny pillow, my lips still tasting hers. 'Schrooms can do that, turn you into a lazy traveler, floating on a raft – or an old gyno table – as time carries you along like a slow-moving river.

I'm not sure how long I've been happily Huck Finning when my wits begin to whisper from somewhere inside my head. They remind me it's Thursday night and I'm supposed to be working.

I struggle to stand, my lower back all prickly pins and needles. I can walk only if I'm listing forward about 30 degrees. Outside the doctor's office, I lumber down a dark hallway, like some Frankenstein figure, my arms outstretched, fingers brushing the walls for balance.

There are voices behind Roddy's door and a halo of golden light shimmers around the edges. I stand outside for a long moment, slowly bringing myself erect and turn the handle.

What I see through the open door almost drops me back to the floor.

Bathed in celestial light, Kathy poses nude on a pedestal draped in white satin. Two photographer's lights reveal every glowing inch of her – her back arched, her knees bent under her, her head tilted, staring right at me, the pillow lips set in a Mona Lisa smile. The boobs, not a tan line in sight, push toward the ceiling like two freshly sprouted mushroom caps tipped in pale pink.

It's a full minute before I see anything else in the room. But eventually I notice Roddy holding a Nikon. He's kneeling, trying to

32

focus. Across the room, Carl stands in front of a framed canvas on an easel, applying broad strokes of honey-colored paint. Kathy's white robe is tossed over a chair in the far corner.

"Hi, Buzz Man, how you doin'?" Kathy asks, without moving her pose or her lips much. "Roddy, can we break?"

Roddy nods and flips off one of the lights. Kathy unspools from the pose. I watch her slip into the robe, my heart hammering inside my chest.

Roddy hands me my backpack as Kathy disappears into the next room.

"Hope you don't mind, but I took care of business for you," Roddy says. "I got mine, Carl took his and I called Rexie, who stopped by and picked up his. The money's in the front pocket."

I unzip the backpack and poke my hand into the large back pocket. One lid left.

"Anybody know what time it is?" I ask. "I'm due at El Goya before 10."

"You've got five minutes," Kathy says, emerging from Roddy's kitchen, handing me a small tumbler with two inches of brown liquid at the bottom. "Drink this first. It'll settle you down."

I tilt back the glass and feel the warm bourbon settle like a fuzzy puppy in my stomach.

"Drop in again sometime, Buzz Man," Kathy says.

Her voice sounds like she's purring.

"I'll keep my window open."

***

The door to Upstairs South opens onto Seventh, and I ease out slowly, my head emerging first, scanning the street for killers or cops. The coast, as they say, is clear. A block away, just past the Ritz marquee, is the ornate brick and marble palace that is *El Goya*. Calling *El Goya* a gay nightclub is just wrong. It's more like a gay mall - six themed bars, a dance dungeon, and a twice-a-night drag show, starring several of my best customers.

I know I'm late and Helga will be boiling, but as I start to walk I can't seem to pick up any speed. Maybe it's the bourbon, on top of the 'schrooms, but the knots of people headed into the club and the cars circling the block, all seem to be moving in Fast-Forward, while I'm in Slow-Mo.

I manage to limp across Fifteenth to the wide alley behind *El Goya*. It's the only alley in Ybor that doesn't seem like a potential crime scene. After arsonists from a competing gay bar tried but failed to torch the place, the Goya's owners added prison-yard security lights and Jesse, a former professional wrestler who sits outside the stage door, with a shiny pistol in a black holster.

"Buzz Man," he says, ebony skin reflecting the klieg lights, "She's been out here three times lookin' for your ass. You best take care of business or even I won't be able to protect you."

He grins and pulls open the door. I stumble into a hallway lit by dangling bare bulbs, and echoing with a bass heavy version of Rick James' *Superfreak* – *"She's a very kinky girl…"* The dressing rooms are just a few steps away and I can hear Helga Heinie's smoky tenor behind the closed door.

"I don't care how many fucking tourists are in the seats – I'm done with this shit," Helga shouts. "Those bitches can introduce themselves. I'm walking out that door and going directly to Village Inn for a goddam Greek omelet, and I'm not coming back."

"Did I tell you I got a call from Trixie the Trannie last night?" I hear Angel say. "She's moving back from Atlanta and wonders if that old bitch Helga has finally hung up her high heels and moved to Sun City. Her words, of course, not mine."

Angel, the show's choreographer, is a wisp of a man and a lover of show tunes, who spends most evenings fighting with his hulking headliner. He usually wins.

I knock on the door.

Helga yanks it open and there she is - all six-feet-six of her in full regalia: black eyeliner, black lipstick and black curls falling from a World War I Prussian helmet, with the spike on top; black leather bodice laced over her very formidable fuselage. She slaps my shoulder with a riding crop.

"Where the hell have you been? This fuckin' ship is ready to set sail and I got no buzz, Buzz."

I smile but doing that saps the last of my energy. I sink slowly to my knees.

"Buzz Man? You okay?" Helga is suddenly over me sounding a lot like a female impersonator version of my mom when I'd wake up with the flu. She lifts me without strain and sets me down in an upholstered chair.

"Rough night," I whisper. "Check the backpack."

Helga finds the baggie and tosses it to Angel, who pulls out a fat bud. Helga hands him a mahogany and brass bong – ordered special from Amsterdam – and Angel starts to fill it.

"Angel, find me a goddam light," Helga hisses.

"Find it yourself. Do I have to do everything around here?"

I manage to pull the Zippo from my pocket and raise it up with a quivering arm.

In seconds, Helga is blowing smoke in my direction. Angel slips out to start the pre-show music.

"Poor baby," says Helga, giving my face a soft slap. "You need a little pick-me-up."

She retreats to her Art Deco dressing table, checking her makeup in the big round mirror. She turns back to me, waving two twenties. She stuffs them in my pants pocket, along with my Zippo, then she leans into my face.

"This'll get you back on your feet."

I hear the snap of an amyl nitrate caplet and feel the hot vapor steaming up my nose.

"See ya next week!" Helga hollers, as she runs out the door. "And next time, don't keep this bitch waiting!"

It's like someone has attached a battery charger to my heart and given me a jump.

I almost leap from Helga's chair.

My wits, which had taken a long coffee break, get back to work.

If I get home right now, I can probably talk Barry into going back to *El Sama* and throwing some pots for a few hours, or going to Rough's for the late night Happy Hour, or driving over to Cocoa Beach to watch the sunrise. Something! Anything!

In the dark hallway, I hear Helga starting the show - "How many times this month has this first nasty bitch been to the clinic for a penicillin booster? Gotta be sixteen, going on seventeen. Please put your legs together for *El Goya's* favorite Swissssssss Missssssssss-stake – Maria Von Tramp!"

***

It just makes sense that I get back home as quickly as possible. There's so much I could be doing. I laugh at the thought of the cops trying to grab me now – my backpack clean enough to pass through Customs.

For safety, I've stashed the cash down my pants, so the Marielitos can go fuck themselves.

And there's no pain in my back at all. In fact, I can't really feel my feet as they slap the hex-block sidewalk along Seventh. I'm moving in Fast-Forward now - thinking about Kathy and Roddy, and Frankie and Josh, Helga and Angel, even Barry, and this incredible old hulk called Ybor City.

I pull out my Zippo and snap back the lid. When the flame catches, I raise my arm – tipped in fire - toward the heart of the moonless Ybor night.

The Buzz Man is the master of this entire fuckin' disaster!

The paw on my shoulder arrives so swiftly and with such force that I don't realize what's what until I'm deep in a dungeon of an alley with my back flat against the wall. I actually giggle, thinking one of my pals is about to stuff a joint in my mouth.

"Barry, is that you, ya bastard?"

"Fuego?"

The voice is a smooth, almost-effeminate tenor.

My eyes blink furiously but can't gain any traction in the blackness. Someone is close, pressing me into the bricks. I feel a mitt of a hand against my shoulder. The breath in my face stinks of stale beer and rotten eggs.

"Fuego?" the voice repeats, still a request, not a command.

My heart bangs in my ears. Still holding the Zippo, I snap the ridged wheel, throwing off sparks, but it doesn't catch.

In the spark-light an image appears – not my assailant, but Frankie dark and handsome, wrapped in a towel at his front door – "Buzz Man, you're late."

A lazy, bottom-of-the-well-burp coats my face in a spicy rub of onions, garlic and black beans.

"Fuego?" the voice asks again.

I flick my thumb and in the spark Roddy leans over me – "Buzz Man, you okay?"

I shake my head hoping my wits will somehow rattle into place. Tires screech in the distance and I catch a snippet of *Superfreak* – *"The kind you don't take home to motha!"*

Another snap of my thumb and the Zippo presents a tapering two-inch flame, all reddish orange on the edges and steel blue at the base.

In the glow I fall deep into Kathy's slate gray eyes. I press my own eyes shut and shake my head again.

I feel a hand pulling the Zippo's flame closer. A man's face comes into focus - it's coffee-colored velvet, trimmed in tight black curls. Sprouting from two pencil-thin lips is the mahogany trunk of an unlit cigar.

The face leans in. The Zippo's flame caresses the trimmed tip of the cigar. The man puffs once, twice, three times - smoke clouding up the narrow space between us. He takes one more long, deep drag, the cigar's tip coated in glowing sparkles, then exhales into my face.

He slowly unlocks the flaming Zippo from my fingers, flipping the lid shut with a clink.

"*Gracias*," he says, waving the lighter and stepping back slowly, his chamois-soft face sinking beneath the surface of the shadows.

He turns and I watch the flat back of him dissolve into the darkness, leaving behind only a rising cloud of pale white smoke.

RED LETTER

The cap should have been the easiest part – a patch of dark cotton attached to narrow straps that hung from each side, so you could tie it below your chin.

The dress and underskirts had been easier. The heavy cotton hung well and didn't fight the needle. The Puritans spurned buttons, preferring string and simple bows, perfect for her needs. One strong pull and the entire bodice opened up.

But there were no patterns for the cap. And it had to fit her head just right - enough to hide her thick blonde hair, but not mash it so badly that it was matted when she yanked off the cap, swung it over her head a few times, then let it fly.

Two failures taunted her from the trashcan next to the sewing machine. Paige could stay calm during major catastrophes, but wasting fabric put her in a foul mood. Time to take a break. She'd been at it for over an hour and her fingers were sore, her back starting to stiffen. Besides, Pearl would be up soon, playing her Charlie Brown Christmas record at full volume on this warm May morning, and demanding toasted Cuban bread wet with melted butter.

Paige stretched, her long torso arched, her arms skyward, not sure if she was hearing the muted snap of her vertebrae or just feeling them clunking into place like ungreased gears. That's when the tiny brass bells looped along a leather cord – her improvised doorbell – begin to jingle.

The young woman on the sidewalk could have stepped off a cigar box label: a pale, milkmaid face; a cotton sundress revealing a sliver of cleavage; shoulder length black curls rustled by a soft breeze and haloed by the morning sun. For an instant, Paige thought a celestial creature had fallen to earth outside her house. She decided she was just dizzy from the stretch.

"Are you Hester?" asked the woman, pointing to the sign by the door written in an "Olde English" script – **Hester Prynne, Sewing and Alterations**.

Paige stood mute, her brain searching for words that didn't come.

The Hester sign had been a joke – mostly. After she restored the building in Ybor City, a place just outside the Abrams' "250-mile exclusion zone," Paige thought of Hester, exiled to the outskirts of her city and trying to support her child doing sewing jobs. So far, Paige's only customers were drag queens from *El Goya*, the gay

41

nightclub around the corner, and they apparently didn't get the joke.

Angel, the show's elfish choreographer, had arrived first, holding a rhinestoned Cher pantsuit that needed a hem. He returned the next day with a form-fitting Diana Ross gown with a busted zipper – "Our Diana has to step away from the black beans and rice or switch to Rosemary Clooney." Next came one of the stars, Maria von Tramp, long and lean, dressed down for daytime in faded denim and a Talking Heads T-shirt, the only giveaway to her diva status a light coating of foundation, pale pink lipstick, a silk scarf wrapped Grace Kelly-like around her blond curls, and a $15 Chanel purse from the open-air market on North Boulevard.

"We're doing *The Sound of Muzak*," Maria whispered, in a feminine baritone. "Got any ideas?"

After Paige delivered a breakaway nun's habit, she became the unofficial costumer of the *El Goya* drag show.

But today's customer didn't need makeup or costumes to pass as female. She was clearly the real thing.

"Hope I didn't screw the pooch," the milkmaid said. "I'm so ding-y sometimes. Am I in the right place? Sewing? Alterations?"

She lifted a canvas bag; the scalloped edges of skirts pushed out between the straps, a bouquet of silk and satin.

"Yes. Sewing," Paige stammered.

"And you're Hester? Like in the book?"

"Sort of. Sorry. It's kind of a…"

Paige stammered, trying to think. Even now, after all that had happened, hearing those tiny bells jingling reminded her she was still expecting something. She just wasn't sure what it was.

There was no way to explain all that to this beautiful stranger, so she just said: "I'm Paige. Paige Young. The Hester thing…it's kind of an inside joke."

In high school, when her parents' domestic thunderstorms rolled through, Paige would retreat to her bedroom, sharing a single mattress with heroines of the tragic variety - Madame Bovary, Lady Chatterley, *Dr. Zhivago's* Lara, and Hester. Reading Hawthorne's tale during her junior year at Coral Gables High she couldn't imagine a world like Hester's. Just one year later, with a baby growing inside her, she could picture herself on a plank platform before jeering neighbors, cradling her illicit infant, a large red "A" covering her milk-swollen breasts.

Miami in 1981 had little in common with Boston in 1640, but shame and condemnation have never belonged to just one century. At least Hester loved Dimmesdale. Paige liked Ezra, but she was always sure that what she felt for him wasn't love.

Until things started with Ezra Abrams at the beginning of senior year, boys were a foreign land she had no interest in visiting. When Ezra suggested they go out sometime, Paige asked, "Are you sure?"

"I mean, if you're not busy," Ezra said, his mitt of a hand on Paige's open locker door.

This was the first time she'd been asked out, and Paige was pretty sure the rules she learned reading Pride and Prejudice didn't apply.

"I could probably get away sometime. When?"

"Tonight?"

"I study dance. Tonight, I mean…"

"Great. Tomorrow night then?"

"Uh…Ok."

Paige felt her cheeks reddening. Ezra flashed a toothy smile like a salesman who had just closed a deal. She half-expected him to shake her hand.

As a gawky adolescent with glasses, and a mouth full of metal, Paige hadn't had to worry about boys and dates. But sometime around the end of junior high and the beginning of high school, her mismatched features, her tomboy torso, and her bony elbows and knees morphed into something beautiful.

Paige hadn't seen the changes that way. Standing naked in front of her mother's full-length mirror, she was embarrassed by this new version of herself. She bought larger patterns for her homemade outfits, burying her curves in dresses with high collars and full skirts.

She settled easily into the role of the high school oddity. While other girls traded glasses for colored contacts, Paige tucked her thick bifocals into thrift store black frames from the '50s. She wore no makeup, left her legs and armpits unshaved, and kept to a daily beauty routine of Ivory soap and warm water and finished it all off by yanking her hair into a tight bun. She contributed poems to the literary magazine and danced in the chorus of Guys and Dolls. As she started her senior year, she counted just one friend – a wisp of a boy named Sam Saul. Cast as Nathan Detroit, Sam bragged that he had found the "gay undertones" in his character.

"Of course he didn't want to marry Adelaide. He totally had the hots for Sky Masterson," he explained to Paige.

Sam did not have the hots for Ezra: "That nose. Those teeth. Plus, there's Jewish and TOO JEWISH. His family is totally TJ. You'd be good breeding material but – oops, wrong tribe."

Sam was right about Ezra's looks. Ezra wasn't handsome, but he was solid and masculine, and at least two inches taller than Paige. Literally a big man on campus, Ezra played basketball and was president of the Key Club. The only child of a wealthy Orthodox family who kept Kosher, he grew up in a landmark 1925 Mediterranean castle on Alhambra Circle. Paige lived less than a mile away, in a squat 1940s box on Mendoza Avenue. While their houses

were close, Ezra Abrams and Paige Young could have been planets
circling different stars.

After that first date – a sunset walk through Coconut Grove's
waterfront park - Ezra pursued Paige with late-night phone calls,
hand-written letters and wrapped gifts she actually wanted: a first
edition of Catcher in The Rye, knit shawls from a family trip to Israel,
boxes of Belgian chocolate truffles given to a girl who thought a
Whitman's Sampler was an expensive treat.

"You're his shiksa goddess," Sam told her.

"What's that?"

"You're the Presbyterian girl he sleeps with on his summer
backpacking trip before he comes home and marries Shoshanna."

***

The milkmaid's name was Vivica and she danced in the flamenco
show at the Columbia Restaurant in Ybor.

"Our seamstress ran off with a weak-chinned waiter to East
Bumfuck," said Vivica, who balanced her peasant girl looks with a
city girl's vocabulary. "The little bitch gave us no warning. Luckily,
somebody saw your sign."

While the rest of Tampa's immigrant district was emptying out, the
Columbia, a cluster of ornate dining rooms founded by Ybor
immigrants in 1905, continued to draw crowds for *arroz con pollo,*
frijoles negros and a floor show featuring a live band and a flamenco
troupe. The show schedule – two a night, six nights a week - took a
toll on the costumes now piled onto Paige's sewing table.

Paige shifted through the scallops of satin, silk and polyester, finding
rips and pulled hems, but nothing she couldn't handle. She was
embarrassed that she'd been in Ybor over two years and hadn't
ventured the few blocks to the Columbia.

"Hey, don't worry," Vivica said, after Paige apologized. "It's a good show though we mostly play to tourists and old fart birthday parties. But where else in Tampa can a dancer make a living without showing her coochie?"

Paige smiled and wondered if maybe she should consider a flamenco class.

Just then, she heard the Linus and Lucy theme; five months after Christmas, Vince Guaraldi's low-key holiday jazz remained on Pearl's turntable, even serving as musical background for the family Seder. In deference to Pearl's father, Paige was serving her daughter a full religious smorgasbord.

The child trotting down the stairs was a three-year-old version of Paige, all porcelain and blonde, in a well-worn pink tutu, ballet slippers and a plastic tiara set with rhinestones – her daily outfit for the past two months. Pearl ran directly to her mother's guest and took her by the hands.

"You like toasted Cubans?" Pearl asked Vivica, loud enough to be heard a block away.

"Not really. I'm pretty sure I dated one in 1979 and he wasn't much fun," Vivica told her.

"It's a breakfast food!" Pearl shouted, setting the stranger straight. "You want some?"

"I would, but a girl's got to watch her figure. I'm a dancer, like you," Vivica said.

"And like Mommy!" Pearl announced.

"Modern? Ballet?" Vivica asked, eyeing Paige with a new curiosity.

"Exotic, I'm afraid. But I stop just shy of the coochie."

"Shit, girl. I gotta hear more," Vivica said.

Realizing Pearl was still at her side, the milkmaid's face clinched. "Ooooh. Sorry. My language. I'm not around many kids."

Paige wasn't sure what she wanted from this foul-mouthed stranger, but she knew she didn't want her to leave too quickly.

"I was just about to brew up some café con leche. Can you stay? I'm not around many adults."

***

Astrid Young and her daughter, Paige, managed to stay in the Mendoza house after Philip Young moved to Hialeah with a bartender named Manny. The note her dad tucked into Paige's copy of *Sophie's Choice* said only: "I'm sure you knew this was coming. I'm sorry, sorry and sorry again. When you need me, call and I'll be there." But Paige hadn't known it was coming. She realized she'd been more focused on literary tragedies than personal ones.

As a child, Paige thought her mother was beautiful - pale and blonde, with fine Nordic features, looks she had passed along to her daughter. But as Paige moved from child to teenager, Astrid became a phantom figure, spending most days in her bedroom, complaining of migraines and a chronic intestinal distress her father bitterly labeled "Mother's little helper." After her father left, on the rare days Astrid emerged from her room, Paige thought her mother looked thin and almost translucent, like a leaf plucked from the ground and pressed inside a book.

Her father's job as a draftsman for a small architecture firm never paid much and his monthly support checks soon shrank from four numbers to three and sometimes two. With her husband and his income gone, worry attached itself like a birthmark to Astrid's face.

"What am I supposed to do?" her mother asked one afternoon after school.

47

Paige had no answer. And her mom wasn't really asking – she had already filed the paperwork for welfare and was asking neighbors if they knew any "aggressive" divorce lawyers.

"He wants to 'explore his sexuality?'" she said, her fingers making quotation marks in the air. "Then he has to pay."

Money wasn't something Paige herself worried about. She made her own clothes; the library was free; and she paid for her ballet lessons doing sewing jobs for neighbors. Her teacher, Miss K, was a lithe and beautiful young Russian in the framed black and white performance photos on the walls of her storefront studio. The live version of Miss K, however, resembled a tanned and wrinkled panda tucked into a fuchsia leotard.

"Ms. Young, you have good coordination. And you are good worker. But your body – not a ballet body anymore. Too much body. Too much."

Paige wasn't taking classes with a career in mind. She loved the rigor and precision of ballet, and how she could lose herself inside the movement. So she kept showing up and Miss K kept taking her money.

Money wasn't a big deal for Ezra, and Paige liked that about him. The Abrams' company made trendy junior sportswear in factories in Haiti and the Dominican Republic, clothes that sold cheap in malls around the country. Ezra worked after school at a shipping warehouse near the airport that covered a full city block.

"They think I'm next in line, but I freakin' hate the rag trade," Ezra confessed in a late night phone call. "They've got my entire life already lined up, but I'm not doing it. Listen, keep this to yourself, okay? I'll tell 'em when the time is right. Why cause trouble now, you know?"

Paige promised to keep his secret, even though she wasn't sure whom she'd tell except Sam, who wouldn't care. She also agreed, at

Ezra's suggestion, to keep the budding romance "low key" at Coral Gables High.

Paige, who lived her life in a low key, was fine with that.

Not Sam.

"That's bull pellets," he said. "He just doesn't want it to get back to his family that this gentleman prefers blondes."

"The greatest lovers loved in secrecy," Paige suggested, thinking Romeo and Juliet, Lady Chatterley and her gamekeeper, Hester and Dimmesdale.

"And how well did that work out for them? Girl, do what you want, but promise me you won't sleep with him."

"Don't worry. We're a long way from that."

In truth, the dates had been heating up and Paige hadn't slowed things down. She had wondered what led so many of her favorite characters to risk everything for a few moments of unbridled ecstasy. When Ezra ran his hands under her blouse or pressed a denim-covered knee against her white cotton panties, Paige did feel something urgent bubbling inside her, but when she opened her eyes and looked at Ezra, it felt like research for a novel she didn't want to write.

On a rainy Friday evening in late September, they cruised across the MacArthur Causeway in Ezra's Dad's Mercedes to a Cuban restaurant on Miami Beach.

"Will you go to hell for eating that?" Paige asked, as Ezra devoured a mound of *lechon asado* over yellow rice. "I'm not up on the laws of Judaism, but even I know pork isn't on the good list."

"We're not really a heaven or hell religion," Ezra said, wiping golden drops of garlic sauce off his lips. "But don't worry - I've got lots of guilt. I think it's worse."

49

He laughed and reached across the table, letting his hand brush her cheek.

"You Christians are stuck with the Old AND the New Testaments. I don't know how you even walk out the door without God striking you down," he laughed.

Paige had read the Bible – cover to cover – just like she had read whole rows of the *Harvard Classics* and her Mom's *Time-Life Great Books* series. She liked a good tale with strong characters and the Bible was full of them, but it was also laced with countless rules and regulations.

"I'm worried about Leviticus," she said. "Not so much for me, but, you know, my dad."

"Lots of abominations in Leviticus. My father can quote 'em."

Later that night, in an aging Art Deco hotel, on sheets that smelled like cigarettes, Ezra introduced her to a few abominations. After some initial pain, Paige found the experience pleasant enough, but as Ezra squirmed and gasped on top of her, she couldn't stop thinking about her father, naked and sweaty with Manny.

"We'd make beautiful babies together," Ezra said later, as they lay with their heads close, sharing a pillow. "I mean, not now, but we could."

Like boys, babies were not something Paige thought about much, but she had read enough to know the consequences of all that naked rolling around.

"Don't we need to be careful?"

"We were. I mean, I was. I pulled out before … you know," he hesitated, then he laughed. "Don't worry. It's Old Testament birth control."

Paige didn't remember it from the Bible, but she had read Mary McCarthy's *The Group* and recalled the promise a man had made to a woman after employing *Coitus interruptus*: "There isn't a single sperm swimming up to fertilize your irreproachable ovum."

Art may imitate life, but life doesn't always reciprocate. After two months of Old Testament birth control in Miami Beach hotels, Paige missed her period.

***

"So I did this Isadora Duncan thing for the last *Artists and Writers Ball*," Paige told Vivica, who was still resting her chin on her palm at Paige's kitchen table long after both coffee cups were empty. "I didn't realize that in the spotlight you could see right through my costume."

"Wait, you were the one leading the coronation parade? Oooh...I remember you," Vivica said, her hand coming over to brush Paige's arm.

"Anyway, afterwards, this guy in a Colonel Sanders outfit gave me his card. It was for a strip club named *Scarlet's*. It seemed like a sign."

Paige was surprised to hear herself talking so easily with this stranger. It wasn't her way, but she didn't want Vivica to leave, and so she kept talking. She told her how the decision to dance at *Scarlet's* hadn't been too tough. *Flash Dance*, the hit film of 1983, had spurred a demand for sexy dancing with a storyline. Paige had lots of story lines and 15 years of dance classes. She also had a child to support.

"I had just finished Maria's breakaway nun's habit and I thought, this could be something. So I called the guy. I told him I would only work there if I could do it my way, dancing as characters from books I loved."

"But the naked part, for me that's the fuckin' deal breaker," Vivica said, whispering the curse word so Pearl, who was sprawled on the

51

wood floor, furiously adding crayola colors to a black and white Haggadah left over from last month's Seder.

"After the first time, it's not that hard. And I feel like it isn't me up there but someone else."

Working Thursday and Friday nights, and dancing only on stage, Paige was quickly taking home $1,000 a week, enough to pay her bills and send Pearl to an expensive pre-school. After a few weeks, Paige's appearances were advertised on the marquee outside under her stage moniker – "Virginia Wolf." She kept the misspelling because the guy who stuck the plastic letters on the marquee insisted he didn't have another "O."

She told Vivica about Lolita, Lady Chatterley, and the biblical temptress Bathsheba, prowling the club's stage in costumes Paige sewed herself.

"You're delivering culture to the horny masses," Vivica laughed. "It's very noble. Imagine all those guys going home and whacking off to the classics."

Paige described how some of the dancers were convinced Madame Bovary was the proprietress of a high-end brothel – "We don't get many librarians at the strip club."

"Don't tell anyone, but I'm not working with any Fulbright scholars at the flamenco show either," Vivica said. "But Hester? They must have liked her. Everyone knows that fuckin' shame story."

"I've been waiting on Hester. I want to do her justice," Paige said. "I was working on the costume today. But I'm having trouble with her cap. And I need a good idea for how to do the red letter."

"Maybe I can help you with that," Vivica said.

***

Ezra's family had not been happy with the news of her "condition" –

at least that's what Ezra told her. Paige wasn't invited to meet them.

As word spread at Coral Gables High about the odd girl in the homemade dresses who seduced Ezra to get at his family's money, Paige became a target.

It was late February and Paige's pregnancy was still well hidden beneath her loose-fitting dresses. But as she carried her tray through the crowded cafeteria, eight girls rose in unison from their table and followed her. Paige saw that they were dressed exactly alike – madras slacks, soft blouses with Peter Pan collars buttoned to a neck wrapped by a single strand of pearls. They had obviously rehearsed their song – a Rod Stewart hit called *Tonight's the Night*.

Come on angel my hearts on fire
Don't deny your man's desire
You'd be a fool to stop this tide
Spread your wings and let me come inside.
Tonight's the night....

"Screw 'em," Sam said after the singing stopped and Paige sat beside him, blinking back tears. "We should get matching letter sweaters. A pink "Q" for me. A scarlet "A" for you."

Ezra wasn't around to tell the real story. His parents had moved him to a private high school.

"It's complicated," Ezra told her, during a late night phone call a few days after Paige's shame serenade. It was his first call in over a month. "I'm working on my parents. I told them I was going to marry you and that's that."

"Is that what you want?" Paige asked.

"I just need a little time. OK?"

"Take all the time you need," Paige said.

The pregnancy was something she saw as hers, not something she was sharing with Ezra. As for the future, she was sure a resolution was coming. She just didn't know exactly what it was.

The week after Ezra told his parents, a letter arrived for Paige at her house. Inside was $3,000 in cash and the business card of an obstetrician in Coconut Grove. When Paige called, the doctor's receptionist told her all her medical expenses had been pre-paid.

She didn't tell Ezra or her mother about the letter. Astrid didn't even know Ezra's last name and Paige refused to share it.

Still, her mother insisted they consult a lawyer, perhaps the bulldog she had hired to extract more money from Paige's father. Paige's father's departure had seemed to give Astrid a new purpose. She rose early and made lists at the kitchen table, determined Philip would pay dearly for leaving them alone on Mendoza Avenue.

Paige insisted that no lawyers were needed.

"It's complicated," she told her mother. "But don't worry."

"Men need to support their families," Astrid said, looking up from a yellow legal pad. "They can't just do whatever they want."

Paige hid the $3,000 under her mattress and on the first of each month she left $400 on her mother's nightstand. They never spoke about it, but the money was always gone the next day.

Her relationship with Ezra was now confined to sporadic late-night phone calls.

"My father thinks God is testing him," Ezra said, his call coming after midnight. Paige had been asleep for two hours.

"Like Job?" Paige yawned.

"More like Abraham and Isaac."

"Ah, the Binding of Isaac. God wants your Dad to kill you to prove his faith?"

"I thought only Jews called it 'the binding,'" Ezra said.

"I'm becoming a Jewish scholar in my spare time."

Paige had spent most of April and May in the library. After a five-day stretch when she arrived at school each morning and found "SLUT" painted in red lipstick on her locker, she had been offered the opportunity to "complete her studies at home." At a tiny desk tucked deep in Coral Gables' modern fortress of a library on Segovia Street, Paige rotated her reading time between tracts on Judaism and books like "*What to Expect When You're Expecting*." Paige's family was vaguely Protestant, but she didn't feel bound to any particular religion and her child would be equal parts Jewish and Gentile.

So she read Bible stories aloud – David and Goliath, the parting of the Red Sea, Moses in the bulrushes - assuming the girl child living in her belly was listening. She had also chosen a name - *Penina* - a Yiddish word for purity and inner beauty. The English translation was "Pearl." The fact that Pearl was Hester's daughter's name only confirmed Paige's decision.

"My father says I need to think about the big picture," Ezra said.

"What picture is that?"

Before he could answer, Paige heard something from Ezra's room – a door opening, a hissing whisper – then, the dismissive drone of the dial tone.

As Paige drifted back into sleep, she knew she wouldn't have to figure out how she really felt about Ezra.

***

"So…what did you think?" Vivica asked, appearing in full costume and makeup at the table Paige and Pearl were sharing next to the Columbia stage. She curled into an empty seat.

"I love the flamingo!" Pearl shouted, as Paige put her finger to her daughter's lips.

"We'll have to get you some lessons," Vivica told her, reaching out, her red-tipped fingers rustling Pearl's hair.

"Maybe me too?" Paige said, her eyes meeting Vivica's. "It was…sad and beautiful. I loved it. Thanks for inviting us."

After stopping by every morning for two weeks, bringing a repair job or a loaf of fresh Cuban bread from La Segunda Bakery, Vivica had arranged for Paige and Pearl to see the Columbia flamenco show.

It was Tampa in 1983, but they could have been in Havana in the 1950s. A trio of aging musicians in tuxes warmed up the crowd with mambo versions of jazz standards. Vivica's costumed flamenco troupe pounded the stage in duos and trios. And finally, there was Cesar Gonzmart, the aging but regal owner, in a perfectly fitted tux, his ebony hair slicked back and curling around his collar, playing a slow bolero on violin, leaning over his customers, his bow slicing just above their heads.

As Gonzmart stepped off, waving his bow to acknowledge the applause, Vivica strode into the spotlight for her solo.

She looked nothing like the young milkmaid who had visited Paige's kitchen. She could have been wearing a mask - powdered cheeks, crimson lips, tendrilled lashes. Her red dress, scooped deep in the back, stuck to her bodice like a second skin. The scalloped skirt was loose. She lifted and turned it, so the ruffles swelled and collapsed like waves on the ocean.

Disconnected somehow from her pounding heels, Vivica's upper body undulated –Paige imagined a cobra rising from a basket. The other dancers, now circling the stage, clapped in double time. Vivica's arms swayed like reeds brushed by an evening breeze, her eyes searching in vain for someone just out of sight.

There were tragic echoes of all Paige's literary heroines – their love, loss, desire, grief – carved into Vivica's flamenco facade.

Moments later, the show ended with a full-cast finale, all thundering feet and clicking castanets. When the applause died out and the stage lights dimmed, Paige felt like she'd been holding her breath. Pearl, who had danced on her chair during the entire show, looked over at her mom and hollered "Whew!" She ran a tiny hand over her forehead, pretending to wipe away beads of sweat.

Paige leaned over and kissed her daughter, and suddenly, there was Vivica, brushing Pearl's hair, sitting so close Paige could smell her sweat mixed with patchouli.

Paige laid her hand on the table next to the flickering candle and met Vivica's eyes, still partially hidden behind fan-like lashes.

Vivica's fingers eased away from Pearl's hair and lit, light as a dragon fly, on Paige's upturned palm.

***

It was August of 1981 when Paige met the lawyer at McDonald's on U. S. 1, a few miles from her house. Pearl was one-month old, Paige just two months past her eighteenth birthday. For the meeting, Paige chose a white shirt-waist dress that buttoned to the collar and fell to the middle of her calves. She added a choker of fake pearls borrowed from her mother.

The man waiting at a table in a side area near the bathrooms was bone-thin, his skin chalky, his face hidden beneath a thick, salt and pepper beard and a flat-brimmed black fedora. A dark, pin-striped jacket hung on him like a cloak.

Paige thought he could have been a man from another time, except for the extra large carton of French fries on the table, and the crimson alp of ketchup rising from a flattened-out hamburger wrapper.

When Paige approached, the man didn't stand or offer his hand. He barely looked up at her. Instead, he indicated with a slight bend of his wrist that she should sit down.

When she did, he lifted a legal-sized manila envelope and set it carefully on Paige's side of the table.

He sat silently – occasionally chewing a fried finger of potato tipped in red - while Paige turned through five pages of clauses and sub-clauses, including clause 12-A that required "The Aforementioned Paige Young" to live at least 250 miles from Miami.

"It is simple, really," he said, as Paige set the papers back on the table. His voice was smooth and round, carrying what seemed like a thousand of years of authority, diminished only slightly by the floret of ketchup blooming on his lower lip. "The Abrams family takes no responsibility for your child. However, if you agree to the terms, a one-time financial gift will be made to you. This offer is good today only."

His finger pointed to a sum at the bottom of the fifth page: $175,000. Below the figure was space for Paige's name and a date.

"So about that 250-mile clause…I'm not great at geography but doesn't that mean that Cuba and most of the Caribbean are off-limits?" Paige asked, smiling at what she thought was a small joke. The man's expression didn't change.

"It means what it means."

He pulled a sleek silver pen from his pocket and slid it toward Paige. Tiny black letters embossed on the shaft spelled out Miami International Sportswear.

"Ezra's okay with this?" Paige asked. It had been three months since his last phone call.

"No one is okay with this, but this is what it is."

58

A family – a mother, father and a skinny pre-school girl – pushed into the next table. While Paige watched, the child said something in Spanish that made her parents laugh. When Paige turned back to the lawyer he was staring at her, the sagging skin shrouding his weary eyes dripping like candle wax, the speck of ketchup still clinging to his lip.

Paige leaned toward the family at the next booth.

"*Una servilleta?*" she asked, in halting Spanish.

The little girl handed her a napkin.

Paige thanked her and reached suddenly across the table, pushing through the bushy beard to wipe the ketchup off the lawyer's lip.

The man leaned back in his seat, his eyes going wide. Paige showed him the red mark on the napkin.

"You had a little schmutz," she said.

Paige pulled the silver cap off the pen and wrote her name and the date in bright blue ink.

***

Staring into a large mirror framed by golden bulbs in tight wire cages, Paige adjusted the cap gently over her hair.

Her mirror image seemed out of place in a dressing room crowded with painted women in leather boots, polyester lingerie and feather boas. Paige was a picture of the good Puritan woman – dark cotton dress, laced up the front, no makeup, her hair in a bun, the simple black bonnet tied primly below her chin.

She wondered what her parents would think if they saw her in this dressing room or later, on a stage with a silver stripper pole in the center.

Her father had visited a few weeks after she bought the building in Ybor.

When she had greeted him at her door, he was thinner than she remembered, his hair bleached blond, a diamond stud in his left ear. But Philip Young was still as quiet and introspective as his daughter. He stayed for a week in her empty building, sleeping, like Paige and Pearl, on air mattresses. He helped Paige manage the needs of a new baby, and designed a floor plan for the renovation. Friends of his in Miami recommended a Tampa contractor.

"How's Manny?" Paige asked, while they ate burgers at an Ybor pub called Rough Riders.

"Gone," her father said. "But it's okay."

"You aren't going back home, are you?"

"I'm not that guy anymore," he said.

They were quiet for moment, then he spoke up.

"Speaking of that guy, do you hear anything about Pearl's father?"

She told him Sam and Ezra were classmates at Brandeis. Sam had called a few weeks ago with news: his gay adaptation of The Odd Couple was being work-shopped in the drama department – "Oscar's a bear, all big and hairy. I play Felix. Typecasting or what?" – and, oh, yes, Ezra was officially engaged to Rachel Weinstein, of Long Island, New York.

"Paige," Sam had almost shouted, "she's totally TJ!"

Her only call from her mother came a few months later, after the crews had finished restoring the building. A week earlier, Paige had mailed a cashier's check for $70,000 - all the settlement money she had left after the building project.

Her mother did not mention the check.

"So, are you coming home sometime?" Astrid's voice sounded distant and thin.

"It might be a while," Paige said. "I'm trying to get established here. But I've got a spare room. You could come visit and see Pearl."

"I don't think I can travel right now. My stomach…you know?"

Paige told her the invitation was always open.

That was almost two years ago.

Paige hadn't told Joe Rodriguez, but this would be Virginia Wolf's last show at Scarlet's. She could pay her bills with the sewing business, especially now that she and Vivica were sharing living expenses. And she'd been promised an audition for the flamenco show, after she'd finished a few more private dance lessons.

So Hester was her finale. The end of a very long story.

Staring at the pious face in the mirror, Paige shut out the chattering dancers and the distant thump of disco music. Like that young girl who hid in her bedroom, living alongside her tragic heroines, she let Hester's last dance unfold in her imagination.

She could see it all:

The DJ spins a slow-boiling gospel number that builds to a religious frenzy. During the quiet opening, Hester steps demurely onto the stage. Customers and dancers step closer to see this dark Puritan figure gliding between the silver stripper poles – her head lowered, her hands gathered at her waist, palms together, as if in prayer.

Then the beat intensifies, choral shouts building as the underskirts and shawls fall away, leaving Hester in just a bodice, a G-string and the simple cap. Smoke rises around her, gauzy and shimmering in the spotlight.

The men pushing up against the raised runway holler and wave handfuls of bills as Hester pulls her cap loose, flings it around and around, blond curls cascading to the middle of her back.

As the gospel music reaches a call and response crescendo, she jerks loose the laces of the bodice. Hester, liberated now, strides proudly to the center of the stage, where the two runways came together, and waits for the spotlight to find her.

Her arms cross over her chest, her fingers coil around the edges of the heavy cotton bodice. She holds that moment for as long as she can. Then, spinning in a slow circle, Hester rips open the bodice - revealing a single scarlet letter hanging on a simple chain around her neck.

Vivica had known the right designer, an artist on the eastern edge of Ybor who formed letters, bottles and entire menageries of animals from a resin made of sugar and corn syrup that looked exactly like glass.

With all eyes on her, Paige lifts the red letter from around her neck. She holds it above her head for ten long seconds, then hurls it down at her feet, where it shatters into a thousand tiny pieces.

THREE ACTS OF LOVE

ACT ONE

Geishas are dancing in a machine gun nest: three of them, whirling and cackling like Samurai sirens behind stacked sandbags.

"Heerow Yhankee doodle!" one beckons, her accent direct from the dubbed *Godzilla* and *Gamera* flicks I devoured as a kid. "Bring yah Yhankee doodle ovah heah!"

I look around and realize I'm the Yhankee she's after - me in my Dad's steel blue Army Air Corps dress jacket and boxy, billed cap, with the silver eagle on the front. I've raided my parent's cedar closet for a costume party at the old Cuban Club called *Bud Lee's World War Too.*

I'm searching the lobby for Gordo. My pal since kindergarten, Gordo's been dragging me to art district parties lately and I gotta admit, after four years slipping past the velvet rope into one disco dungeon or another, I'm ready for something new. Standing in a 1930s lobby, with dual marble staircases and geometric tile floors, imagining what a Geisha looks like underneath all that makeup and silk, is definitely something new.

"Hey hey Yhankee doodle! Yeah you, Yhankee! Betta rook out!"

Maybe it's the phony Japanese, but suddenly I'm 12 and sitting cross-legged on the floor of our knotty pine Florida room watching another Saturday afternoon creature feature. The black and white skyline of Tokyo on the screen - made from what looks like paper mache and ice cream sticks – awaits the monster that will burn it all down.

A metal rod, pressing hard into my butt, snaps me back.

"Let me see your pass, soldier!"

I turn slowly and I'm staring down the barrel of a toy-store carbine, the kind I carried as a kid in countless backyard wars. The woman holding it is all sharp angles tucked into military green fatigues with a jagged shock of black hair spiking over a face coated in swirling chocolate-brown camo. The black cloth band wrapping her arm carries two white letters: MP.

"Where's that pass?" she barks again, her voice set about four steps lower than other girls.

"I've got it here somewhere," I say, feeling around my pockets. "Not

64

sure where. Maybe you better frisk me."

She spins me around and pushes me roughly against the lobby wall. She swings the rifle over her shoulder and I feel two tiny hands pat their way across my ass.

"Not back here," she says.

"Better try the front pockets."

"You making a lewd suggestion to a superior officer, private?"

I turn and face her. I'm a big guy: six-feet-two, a linebacker in high school. I'm looking down at a toy soldier maybe an inch or two above five feet. Our bodies are close. She's tilted her head back to look at me and just behind her open collar tiny streams of sweat drizzle down her neck.

"So Private Gonzalez," she says. "What are you doing off base?"

"You know my name?"

She pulls the carbine off her shoulder, pushing the barrel into a soft spot a few inches below my belt.

"Robert Gonzalez – goes by Robbie - Chamberlain class of '75? Right?" She asks, still in MP mode.

I nod.

"Well, you're just another grunt to me," she pokes the barrel a little deeper into my groin.

"Please tell me we haven't already dated."

"Not yet."

Lacey Edgerton eventually drops the MP routine and tells me she was a "geeky sophomore" at Chamberlain when I was "that hunky senior." I apologize for not remembering her - "Why would you? I was bones, braces, coke-bottle glasses. The entire disaster."

But a lot has changed with Lacey in five years.

"Robbie Gonzalez. I didn't really picture you as an Ybor kind of guy," she tells me.

"I guess there's a lot you don't know about me."

Best not to say too much at this point. I really don't want Lacey to know I'm a tourist in Ybor tonight.

"I need to record this moment for posterity," Lacey says, as she pulls a Kodak Instamatic from her front pocket and snaps my picture, the flash lingering, making the whole moment glimmer.

"So, you got a phone number? We could catch up." I tell her, pulling out my always-handy Bic.

Lacey thinks for a minute, not saying anything, then she snatches the pen, yanks up my shirt and scratches her phone number on my belly.

I should say here that meeting girls and getting phone numbers is not tough for me. I'm the great-grandson of Spanish immigrants and their dark-haired, swarthy genes have come my way.

I've heard my Mom tell European relatives on long distance: "My son Robert is movie-star handsome."

But for some reason meeting Lacey has me feeling like a pimpled junior high kid getting his first kiss at the school dance while the band plays *Color My World*.

After she marches into the crowd, I rush to the bathroom, where I memorize the reversed three-inch tall digits from the reflection in the mirror. Before I pull down my shirt, something makes me pat the spot where she marked my stomach. I can still feel the sharp tug of the pen on my skin.

Coming out of the bathroom, I spot Gordo in the lobby mob and we adjourn to the basement bar for a beer.

"Another party. More stupid costumes. Man, I'm thinking Ybor is over," he says as we pound down the stairway.

This is pretty much par for the course with Gordo. Instead of "Wittiest Boy" the entry under his picture in the Chamberlain yearbook should have read: "Most Likely To Become A Professional Cynic."

"You remember a girl from Chamberlain – Lacey Edgerton?"

"There was a Lacey in my home room," Gordo says. "Let me think…a little mouse? Likely editor of the literary magazine? Cried into her locker twice a day? Brought her own lunch and always ate alone? That sound like her?"

"Not anymore."

Maybe an hour later, we're back in the ballroom and the party is spiraling toward a crazy crescendo. A couple of hundred GIs, sailors, bobby soxers, and enough "Rosie the Riverters" to build a battleship are bouncing around as a squad of drummers in high school band uniforms pound out a manic march. I spot Lacey on a bench against the rear wall. She's folded onto the lap of a guy with a shock of white-blond hair.

The girl who scrawled her number on my skin an hour ago is now kissing somebody else like she means it.

"You know that guy?" I shout to Gordo, pointing toward the couple.

"That's Jim Rosenquist. The Pop artist. Got a studio in Ybor. And is that…" he shouts back, directly into my ear.

"Lacey…" I nod.

"Well. I guess it's true - the Lord works in strange and mysterious ways!"

I'm feeling a hot spike in my gut, like Lacey is a girlfriend I've caught cheating. But that's crazy. To clear my head, I back out of the double doors and run down the stairs to the lobby leaving Gordo behind. When I step off the landing, I'm face to face with one of the geishas, now out from behind the sandbags and holding a beer. She wraps her free hand around my neck and pulls me close.

"Heerow Yhankee doodle," she whispers, her breath warm on my ear. "Yahnkee ... come home?"

Later, in a shotgun shack on Fifth Avenue, a Yahnkee advances and a Geisha surrenders.

***

For me, Sally Flynn is just about the perfect woman. She has the fresh face of a sorority girl who knows she is pretty but doesn't act like she knows. She reminds me of Judy Varga – we dated in high school – okay, she was the head cheerleader and I was the jock with the letter sweater. What I mean is, Sally is also blonde and athletic and good at what she does, which is being a brand new CPA at Price Waterhouse.

At the moment, her tailored skirt and jacket and starched white business blouse are folded neatly on the chair in my bedroom. We've spent the last hours proving once and for all that even accountants can experience multiple orgasms.

But the real reason I'm smiling as she pulls up the sheet and rests her beautiful head on my shoulder is that she has a boyfriend and he isn't me.

"He says he loves me, but then I don't hear from him for four days in a row," she told me when we met a week earlier at a South Tampa house party. I had listened attentively, nodding in all the right places,

68

while she shared details about her errant boyfriend, who was in the next room with a dozen other guys watching the Phillies take the final game of the World Series from Kansas City.

"Sorry to dump that all on you," she said. I told her I was happy to be her on-call advisor on all things male and gave her my number.

A week later she came to visit, bringing Chinese take-out. I listened and offered a box of Kleenex when the tears fell.

And here we are.

I want to make it clear that I'm a nice guy and what I dislike about dating these days is what happens a day or a week or a month after things reach the naked phase.

Around the time when that cute way she wraps her hair around her index finger, then pulls it into her mouth and starts chewing, begins to drive you nuts. When you ask yourself: Does anyone really need three cats in a one-bedroom apartment?

When she can't understand that when her phone doesn't ring – it's me.

I hate being that guy.

That's why I like this new plan – find girls with bad boyfriends and listen to them. You'd be surprised how many bad boyfriends are out there and how many neglected girlfriends will follow a long therapy session by jumping into bed with their new best friend.

***

The phone connected to the number scrawled on my belly rings for days without an answer.

Then, magically, there is Lacey.

"Ah, my little soldier boy. I wasn't sure if you'd call," she says.

I don't mention my days of dialing. Best to be cool at this stage.

"I thought, you know, for old times sake. Why not? You busy this weekend?"

Lacey suggests we meet Saturday at someplace in Ybor called *El Sama*.

"It's where?" I ask, immediately wishing I hadn't.

"Oh, you never heard of *El Sama*? " Lacey says. "There's this cigar factory on Fourth, it was also a coffin factory and now a bunch of artists work there. Their Halloween party is off the charts."

"My great-grandmother may have rolled cigars there," I tell her. "I never knew exactly which factory, but she and my great-grandfather met in one of those places. If it wasn't for cigars, I might not be here."

"And that would be tragic. So, you wanna go?"

"Where do I pick you up?"

"Soldier boy, you are so old-school. I'll meet you there. And wear a costume. It's a Halloween party."

"It's sounds like fun," I tell her. Before I can get the words out, she's gone, just the drone of the dial tone in my ear.

But a costume party with Lacey does sound like fun and fun is pretty much all I'm into these days. Five months after picking up my marketing degree from the University of South Florida, I'm still living near the campus, in a low-rise complex that horseshoes around a long, palm-lined pool. Some genius named the place *Yella Umbrella* and, yes, the pool umbrellas are the color of ripe bananas. I'm not working, but my rent and bills keep getting paid and my checking account goes *Ka-ching* once a month.

My folks – most likely my mom – have made no move deflate the economic inner tube that keeps me afloat.

At my graduation party, I told Mom I was halfway through writing a self-help book aimed at the flood of baby boomers just leaving college. But the truth is, I haven't gotten beyond the title, "*How To Thrive At 25.*"

Ok. There's a better title out there and I figure that will come once I get some writing done.

Mostly I've been sleeping late, then doing slow underwater laps in the pool, my lungs fat with air, the water cool and heavy on my skin, the pressure humming in my ears like a church choir hitting a single beautiful note. In the afternoon I like to walk around the university without the pressure of classes or a schedule, stopping in the library or the pub. And I spend a lot of nights listening to troubled young women like Sally Flynn who need to get things off their chests – figuratively and literally.

It's a good life.

Now that Lacey is in it, it's even better.

ACT II

Death is waiting for me at the basement entrance of a three-story cigar factory. I'm in the back – a place dark enough for a good mugging - because the street entrance is blocked with ribbons of black duct tape.

Looking up a wall of red bricks, I see colors flashing from a dozen tall second story windows and when I turn, there's Death, in a ground-dragging robe, the single beam of a spelunker's headlamp shining from his cowl like a white eyeball. Death's face is hidden behind a featureless mask and he's holds a scythe – actually a polished hockey stick. He takes my arm and leads me, like I'm Ebenezer Scrooge on Christmas Eve, along a narrow path of lamplight to a battered metal door. Death yanks the knob and the door grinds open with a high-pitched metallic shriek.

A rough push from behind sends me stumbling into a narrow corridor. A bare bulb at eye level swings wildly from a chain, illuminating walls of sallow yellow plaster. When I reach up, I can touch the ceiling and my fingers come back wet. The floor is covered in foam pads, so it feels like I'm walking on marshmallows.

It's all slasher-film scary.

Which is perfect, since I'm hoping I look something like the *Friday the 13th* killer. I've traded the hockey mask for my old football helmet and my green and gold Chamberlain football jersey. I'm carrying a plastic scimitar that a pirate tossed in my direction during last year's Gasparilla parade, Tampa's attempt to mimic Mardi Gras.

The squishy hall opens into a wide basement room where they used to store the tobacco, but now it's thick with ganja smoke, cast red by a couple of gelled spotlights. Somewhere above my head, *Blondie* is singing *Heart of Glass*. I scan for my date but can't see anything too clearly. I pass what could be Superman. There's maybe a gypsy, a nun, and three guys dressed as rabbits.

But no Lacey.

I've brought a six-pack and I'm looking for a cooler and some ice, when I feel something like tiny claws rake across my neck.

Lacey!

"Robbie, is it really you?" Sally Flynn asks. My accountant is a now a kinky Tinkerbell, her wand a cheap back-scratcher with a tiny curled hand at the top – the wooden fingers coated in silver glitter.

"You're in Ybor!" I say, frantically trying to think back to our last conversation. "Where's…uh…Jerry?"

"Dumped! I know you told me to give him some time, but a girl only has so much time, right?"

"Right…"

"And I was having so much fun with you, I thought, who needs that asshole? Feel like dancing?"

"I'm not the world's best dancer."

Sally shouts "*Abracadabra!*" and waves her wand over me.

"Now you're the world's best dancer," she says.

"I guess I can't argue with the wand."

"It's got magic," she says, grabbing my hand.

Moments later, we're upstairs in the colored lights, bouncing around with dozens of costumed characters, as giant speakers blast *Psycho Killer*.

Sally slips the wand into a silk shoulder bag and grabs both my hands – something I really wish she wouldn't do. Holding hands while you dance to the *Talking Heads* is guaranteed to make you look like a dork.

Then, to make it worse, she begins to swing her head madly from side to side. Her face – crowned by a glittering plastic tiara – is one big sorority-house smile. I'm not sure how much of that is actual happiness and how much is post-break up, alcohol-induced euphoria.

This should be a nice coincidence – arriving at a party and tripping into a beautiful, slightly tipsy young woman who knows her way around your bedroom. But since Lacey scratched her digits on my belly, I haven't really thought about any other woman.

After Sally and I dance out the song, she pulls me against one of the support beams rising like tree trunks from the pine floor. She lifts off my helmet and jams her tongue into my mouth. Manicured fingernails climb up the back of my jersey like tiny spiders.

What's a boy to do?

Sally Flynn, once she stops shaking her head like that, is a darn good kisser.

And now I'm wondering if Lacey will actually show up?

The DJ spins *My Sharonna* and I kiss back, swiveling Sally around and pushing her up against the beam, my knee rising into her crisp Tinkerbell tutu.

We dance some more, this time without touching hands, and when Sally isn't looking in my direction, I scan the room for Lacey. At some point, Sally goes in search of a bathroom, and when I turn around Lacey's staring up at me.

"Wow, she's a keeper!"

"Just a friend," I say, hoping she can't hear my pounding heart over the boom of the speakers.

"I remember you were always a friendly guy."

Lacey's costume, if you can call it that, is a collection of black plastic garbage bags tied with twine, leaving lots of skin showing through. The head of a white bristled scrub brush is stuck to the plastic at her shoulder like a corsage. Standing on tiptoes, she manages to get her face close to mine, her breath warm on my cheeks. All I can see now are two luminous eyes and, maybe it's the colored lights, but they seem to be throwing off sparks.

The music seems to fade into the background. Looking down at Lacey I feel like I've taken a blindside hit that popped the wind right out of me.

"I didn't know she was coming..." I manage to say, my head suddenly thick, like it's full of fiberglass.

"Busy later?"

"No. Or yes, with you, I hope."

Her fingers move up, brushing my lips, her mouth at my ear.

"The back door downstairs," she whispers. "At midnight."

Then she's gone and I feel the air returning to my lungs in short, staccato bursts.

***

I don't feel good about what happens next.

Sally says she can't find the friends who promised to meet her at the party, and wherever I move, my crinolined Tinkerbell stays with me, clinging to my arm like a fragrant ball of lint.

So just before midnight, I tell Sally I desperately need to pee and run downstairs to meet Lacey. I find her in the shadows of the basement, passing a joint to Death, who stuffs the flaming stick into a circular opening in his mask, the smoke swirling up inside his cowl.

I grab Lacey's hand.

"We need to go now!"

She wraps her fingers tight around mine and we run laughing through the squishy hallway that leads outside into an October night that still feels like summer.

"I never got around to meditating today," she says, once she's in my car and the AC is blowing. "You mind?"

"Anything you like."

I drive like a madman toward my apartment as Lacey straightens her back, folds her legs beneath her, and brings the palms of her hands

75

together against her chest. When I look over, I see her lips moving slowly, silently. The knot at her shoulder that held two bags in place, has come loose, setting free a tanned teacup of a breast.

I'm doing 80 along the interstate, weaving around slower cars, light poles clicking by like reeds along a wild river, but inside the car, glancing over at Lacey for as long as I dare, the world seems to stand still.

***

Inside my second-story apartment, Lacey looks around slowly, taking in the ivory walls, the white Berber carpet, the teal blue couch, the Ethan Allen recliner, the carved wooden dining table and chairs – all hand-me-downs after my parents remodeled the Carrollwood house.

Suddenly I'm worried that Lacey might not approve.

"We're a long way from Ybor," she says.

"It's just, you know, a place." I manage to say.

"A clean, well-lighted place. My mother would approve," she says.

"Mine does," I tell her, as I take her hand and start to pull her in for a kiss. She eases her fingers from my grip.

"Do you have a T-shirt or something I could borrow? I can't wear these bags another minute."

I go down the hall to grab a shirt. I find her a moment later in the bathroom, all the plastic bags crumpled on the tile floor around her bare feet, as water pounds into the bottom of the bathtub.

That first image of Lacey naked is tattooed onto my brain. She is thin, but her flesh seems deeper than normal skin – firm, yet soft – smoothing out the angles, the arched tracks of her ribs, the sinewy legs that meet at a bloom of thick black curls.

She turns my way as I walk in and reverts to her MP voice.

"Alright soldier. Good job so far. Now go get all your ice trays and bring 'em in here. Double-time, soldier!"

I do as I'm told. Returning with five trays, two old metal ones with pull-handles and three plastic ones you twist to spill the ice. She is sunk down in a tub of cold water; goose bumps bloom across bare shoulders; brown nipples break the surface like volcanic islands.

"All of it," she says, as I dump the trays.

"Aren't you freezing?"

"That's the point of an ice bath. Now get in here!"

I strip and slide in behind her, as the icy water rises to the lip of the porcelain tub and gurgles down the escape drain. The polar plunge and the coppery creature leaning against my chest steal my breath away for the second time in one night.

I'd been optimistic earlier and put fresh sheets on the bed. After we towel off, the sheets are crisp against our cold skin. Lacey pins my shoulders down and climbs on top of me, pressing herself flat across my torso. I feel her breath on my cheek, then she begins to drag her tongue very slowly along my shoulder and up my neck.

The rest of the evening is pretty much what you'd expect if you were expecting a miracle. At some point, I think I hear knocking coming from down the hall, but I am too far away at that moment to pay any attention to the outside world.

Afterwards, as Lacey's breath evens out, I lie on my back and let a bottom-of-the-pool feeling wash over me; I'm pushing through silky water, far below the surface, and I can hold my breath for hours.

I wake early and stand by the bed as thin seams of light seep from the edges of my mom's pleated gray curtains. I stand a long time, admiring Lacey: spikes of black hair on the pillow; sheets pulled around her so tightly I can see every sharp angle.

When I finally break away to start coffee, I remember the late-night knocking and check outside my front door.

Maybe somebody left me a package?

Looking down, I see Tinkerbell's glittery wand broken into pieces on my welcome mat.

***

I think I'm making progress with Lacey even though she still answers her phone only sporadically. And it's only sort-of her phone, she's sub-letting a tiny loft above *La France*, the vintage clothing store on Seventh, while the actual tenant is backpacking through Europe.

She invites me up for our second date. The décor is something between a gypsy wagon and '67 San Francisco – a maroon brocade fainting couch, an antique dressing table with the oval mirror, dozens of long-stemmed candles melted down over silver sticks, and the final touch, thick paisley print fabric covering windowless walls.

Her entire wardrobe seems to come out of a single open suitcase.

On the side tables are gilt-framed color photos of handsome, artsy people in jeans and torn T-shirts smirking at the camera – "my friend's friends," Lacey says.

The only one she claims is a busy black and white in a polished wood frame. She holds it up for me. The picture is odd – I finally realize it's a double exposure and the lone figure in it looks familiar.

"Is that Woody Allen?"

Lacey seems to drift off into the memory.

"He was my hero," she says.

78

"He was?"

"I'm looking for my friend's apartment on the Upper West Side, and this giant Lerch-looking guy keeps trying to talk to me. I see a guy ahead who looks normal enough, so I run up and beg him to walk with me until the creep leaves. That guy was Woody."

"Woody," I say, noting she doesn't use his last name. Like pals.

Lacey says she was taking shots around Rockefeller Center earlier that day and had forgotten to advance the film. So her shot of Woody was a double-exposure, his image going west while all these Manhattan skyscrapers go east.

I'm not really a Woody Allen fan, but I gotta say, Lacey had the perfect shot of the New York City icon.

"So Woody Allen saved you from a giant asshole?" I ask.

"Yeah. He was cool."

"And…"

"We hung out a while."

I don't ask for more details. But it gets me thinking about that other celebrity I saw her with.

Later, sunken into the soft folds of her bed, I hear myself asking, "So what about Rosenquist? You still seeing him?"

I regret it even as I'm saying it.

"Do you see him here now?" Lacey says, her voice taking on an edge.

***

A week goes by and Lacey's phone only rings. I swim furiously each morning, trying to clear her out of my head. Then I stare at the empty page in my typewriter until I can't stand it any longer and I call again.

I've got a book with dozens of names and numbers, but right now, Lacey's is the only one I want to dial. When she finally answers, I'm so happy I almost can't speak.

"Where have you been, soldier boy?"

"Here and there," I manage to say, staying cool. "Doing some work on the book. You know."

"Ah, that book. Building the better boomer. Is that possible?"

"It's tough work, but somebody's got to do it."

"Well, good luck saving the savages. I'm having enough trouble saving myself."

When I get her on the phone, Lacey is always excited and willing, but those days when the telephone phone only rings are killing me. I decide I need to break out the heavy artillery.

That weekend, I drive Lacey up the coast to Tarpon Springs, an old Greek fishing village. I've borrowed my Dad's convertible and after dinner we cruise down a waterfront highway to Crystal Beach. There's a moon blazing down and a path meanders under oaks along a grassy coastline.

I did this exact date with Judy Varga during senior year when I thought I was in love with her. I'd been saving it since then for someone like Lacey.

Lacey is quiet as we walk, watching the moon. I steal glances at this girl who seems to have dropped to the planet from somewhere else. She's wearing a lime-colored Chinese jacket with bones for buttons over black tights and ballet slippers. Somehow, incredibly, she tops it all off with an emerald green beret.

There's a spot where the path opens up at a grassy outcrop just inches above the dark water. Judy Varga went all putty when I sat her there on a night much like this.

We sit and Lacey leans into me as cascades of light dance along the lapping water. I raise her chin and kiss her gently, wrapping my fingers around hers. Damn romantic, I think, but after a minute, Lacey pulls back. She looks at me a long time, the moonlight through the trees painting clusters of leaves across the tiny pyramids of her cheekbones.

Then she slides her hand from my grip.

"Thanks for bringing me here," she says. "Who knew Robbie Gonzalez could be so sweet?"

I feel the steely tip of the knife in my gut.

"Sweet." That's the word lots of girls hear me say just before their phones stop ringing.

ACT III

My mom's heavy curtains keep my bedroom dark, even in the morning. So when I'm awakened by what sounds like a drum solo on my front door, my first look is at the clock. It's almost 11 a.m.

"Shit," I mutter, pulling on some shorts.

I'd gone to bed around midnight, but like every night since that Tarpon Springs date with Lacey, I hadn't been able to fall asleep until almost dawn. It's not like the evening went badly. She seemed happy on the drive home and suggested we spend the night at my place. It ended like it should've – with Lacey, all sweaty after sex, pressed against me as we fell asleep.

But she hadn't picked up the telephone since I'd dropped her off on Seventh Avenue the next morning. That was a week ago.

When I pull open the door, Gordo is outside, all six-feet of him framed in mid-day light.

"Get up, goddammit!" he says, bending down to pick up two Dunkin' Donuts cups at his feet. "I've been calling for three days. I thought you were dead."

"Not dead yet," I tell him, as I take the coffee.

"Bullshit. You're as good as dead. You don't go out. You aren't getting laid. No girl is worth that."

"Maybe this one is."

Gordo's my size and a natural athlete, but in school he couldn't be bothered with practice and pep rallies – "It's a game, man, win or lose everybody on the field will die anyway and nobody will remember the score." His "who cares" attitude grates on me sometimes, but women flock to him. Maybe it's the unshaven beach boy face and his washed-out wardrobe. Today's no exception. He's appeared at my door in   flowered surfer shorts and his standard black t-shirt, this one with John Lennon's face on it.

"Put on your suit. There are five beautiful women lounging around your pool. It's your duty to go down there."

Gordo is exaggerating, but that's his routine. It's the first week of January and the USF students are still on holiday break. The pool is heated, so I can swim laps anytime, but with school out I'm always alone at the pool.

Downstairs I see two girls in sweat suits giggling on chairs set under one of the trademark yellow umbrellas. They look like teenagers who probably snuck in the side gate.

"You need to break out of this funk, my friend," Gordo tells me, as we both lie back on the padded pool recliners, staring up at a cloudless January sky through matching Wayfarers. "What are you doing this weekend? Come with me to New York."

"New York? What for?"

"Planning my escape. Tampa's a dead-end, man. Ybor was cool, but now it's just one big costume party. The East Village. That's the scene I'm aiming for."

"What's wrong with Tampa? They're calling it America's Next Great City."

"You, of all people, should recognize a line of marketing bullshit when you hear it," Gordo says. "Tampa's a strip mall of a town, with signs in empty storefront windows saying 'Coming Soon!' I can't wait that long."

"I don't know. I'm doing okay."

"You're asleep, my friend. You think it's love. It's post-graduation inertia. You need to get moving."

"Maybe I'm happy right where I am."

I'm on my back, staring up from the lounge chair, so I don't notice when Gordo gets up and slips behind me.

Suddenly, I'm moving. Gordo is pushing hard from behind, like my lounge is one of those blocking grids we rammed around at football practice. When the front wheels roll over the pool edge, the whole chaise pivots up sending me into the water, the chair and the cushion following me to the bottom.

I let myself sink all the way down, that beautiful underwater note echoing in my ear. It's nice for a few seconds, then I feel the chair settling slowly onto my back, pinning me to the bottom. Underwater the chair isn't heavy, just cumbersome. I struggle with it a bit, but finally slip free and kick to the surface.

When I come up, I'm gasping and shaking the water from my hair.

"You fucker!" I shout.

Gordo is frowning down from the ledge of the pool deck.

"Consider that your wake up call, my friend," he says. "You can thank me later."

***

Gordo's shock therapy doesn't really take.

Another week goes by. I wake up late on Saturday in bedsheets I haven't changed since the night Lacey was here. I sniff the top sheet, but there's nothing left of her, just the low funk a guy leaves behind after two sweaty weeks of tossing and turning.

There's coffee, but I have to drink it black, since the milk has gone lumpy. Dishes once stacked neatly in my cupboards are unwashed in my sink and stacked on the counter. I eat my last two Pop Tarts with my fingers, standing over the toaster.

I've been passing the long nights watching *Godzilla, Gamera* and *Rodan* destroy Tokyo, and at least a dozen video store cartons – all overdue - are scattered on the floor around my table-top TV.

I dial Lacey's number, counting 25 unanswered rings before I slam the phone down. Five minutes later, I'm in the pool, doing double laps along the bottom, holding my breath until my lungs are screaming and I finally break the surface, gasping.

I do this for an hour, until I've got nothing left. I feel like I did after 60 long minutes of high school football. I linger on the edge of the pool while I get my breath back, counting the rippled lines on the pads of my fingers.

Then, somehow, I'm upstairs at my writing desk, still in my wet bathing suit, staring at the same five words: "*How to Thrive at 25.*"

The ringing phone sounds like a fire alarm. I leap for it.

Lacey!

"Soldier boy. You gonna be home tonight?"

"Why not? You want me to come fetch you?"

I know Lacey doesn't own a car. I doubt she evens knows how to drive.

"No need. See you at 8. Okay?"

When she is gone, I stand up, still holding the telephone. I notice a dozen paths around my apartment, two weeks of repeated steps sunk deep in the matted carpet, like footprints on the beach.

"Get it together!" I shout to the guy standing in a wet bathing suit in the middle of a   trashed apartment. "Fuckin' get it together!"

I race about for two hours – wash the dishes, vacuum the rug, pull dirty clothes from chairs and tables, toss them onto the floor of the closet, then close the doors. I drive to the supermarket to get dinner for two. Lacey doesn't eat meat, which leaves me with one thing I know how to make – cheese omelets.

I buy a bottle of Matous.

I can't remember when I last checked my mailbox. It's an apartment box, set into a metal cabinet of keyed cubbies under the stairwell. When I look today, my slot is stuffed, an envelope edge jutting from the tiny frame, like the hem of a woman's skirt, smashed by a car door.

I sort through the junk mail, the bills and bank statements, and find a large manila envelope addressed to me in my mother's handwriting.

There's no letter inside, just the classified section of the *Tampa Tribune*, opened to the *Help Wanted* section. Under *Marketing and Public Relations* my mother has circled several listings with a yellow marker.

I search the stack of mail for my bank statement and rip it open. No deposit was recorded last month.

***

When Lacey knocks just after 8, I've showered, shaved, and pulled on faded jeans and my last clean T-shirt, one that fits tight around my chest and biceps. My apartment looks perfect - like the first night I brought her home.

"Hey, soldier boy," Lacey says.

I step back as she walks in, just staring at this amazing creature. Tonight she wears a clinging flowered dress that stops just above her knee and the girl who has worn no makeup since I first saw her in black camo has painted her lips bright red. She's even combed her hair straight back, so it curls at the top of her neck.

"It is still Robbie's clean, well-lighted place," she says, looking around at the apartment. "It's nice to be back here."

She takes my hand and leads me to the couch. I pull her close and she comes willingly. I'm suddenly giddy. Maybe the waterfront date two weeks earlier actually did the trick. Maybe we've turned a corner.

But then Lacey pulls back and looks toward my front door.

"I came to tell you I'm moving."

"What?"

"It's kind of sudden, but special. Mark and I are moving to Vermont. There's a farm community. Kind of a spiritual thing."

She starts to say more, but I put my hand over her red lips. I try to say "Who's Mark?" but instead a gasping sob catches in my throat and I feel tears tracking down my cheeks - something that hasn't happened since I tore a groin muscle during a pre-season scrimmage my sophomore year.

Lacey stands up from the couch and reaches out for me.

"Come on," she says.

She leads me like a puppy to the bathroom and turns the spigot. I stand in the doorway as Lacey pulls her dress over her head. She's naked underneath. Her head turns my way.

"Well, are you getting the ice or not?"

After the ice bath, we slip under my fresh sheets, her chilled skin presses against mine and the whole world starts to warm up.

The lovemaking is slow and tender. Whenever I open my eyes, Lacey is staring back at me. Afterwards, she rests her head on my stomach, right where she scrawled her phone number that first night. I wrap my arms around her, my hands pressed against the taut skin of her back. But when she stirs, I don't have the strength to hold her.

"Don't get up," she says, sitting up. "Just let me slip out. It's better."

She is in the bathroom when I get there. I've managed to pull on a pair of dirty gray gym shorts, the laces hanging limp down the front. Lacey is back in the dress and she's pouting in the mirror, so she can get her lipstick on evenly.

She pats my arm as she eases out, going toward the living room.

I follow her there, standing stiff as a statue, unable to speak.

I hear three soft knocks on my door. Lacey walks over and cracks it open, saying something I can't hear to whoever is outside.

Then, she closes the door and walks up to me. I feel her hand soft on my cheek.

"Lacey…" I manage to say.

I feel tears gathering in my eyes and I try to rub them out with my fist.

She pulls the clenched hand away from my face.

"You'll be okay, soldier boy," she says. "You'll thrive. I'm sure of it."

Lacey uncoils my fist, lifts my hand to her lips and carefully kisses each fingertip.

And then, just like that, she is gone.

THE UNDERSTUDY

I blame my band, all of them - Ricochet, Lunar, Kumquat, Speeze. I mean *Saber Tooth* was my idea. And *Zoom My Heart* – MY song - was the closest thing we had to a hit.

"Askin' me how did this love start/One look at her and zoom my heart!"

We closed the show with *Zoom* every night.

I picked the teal satin jackets with the black shawl collars, I got the guys to do the matching feathered pompadours, and I found a mail-order source for those shiny, toe-pinching Beatle boots.

But here I was, dumped in Ybor City in an October that still felt like summer, left behind like the middle child at a gas station stop. I stood on Seventh Avenue watching the van, smoke belching from the tailpipe, pull away for a tour I had booked of North Florida bottle clubs.

I mean, 1985 was going to be our YEAR!

"Salvo, man, I'm sorry but we voted," Speeze said that morning over café con leche at the Silver Ring. "The future is guitars, man. Not keyboards."

What he meant was there are a few more shekels to go around with a four-piece version of *Saber Tooth* than a five-piece.

They chose Ybor as the dumping ground because they knew Sara would take me in. Sara Quell picked me up after our Rough Riders show in August. All that hammering *Saber Tooth* rhythm and the knowing sneer I wear likely did the trick. She had danced in front of my keyboard all night, and was waiting with a beer when we finally crawled off the stage at 2.

Back at Upstairs North, a building she shared with a half-dozen other aspiring artists, actors and writers, we laughed and played like we'd been lovers for years.

The next morning, as I gathered my stuff to catch the van, Sara watched me, sleep still in her eyes, her body wrapped in sheets dotted with tiny flowers.

"You..." I managed to say, as I shook my head in some kind of wonderment.

"I'm thinking maybe we call this love at first night," Sara said.

"Zoom my heart!" I replied, tapping out a staccato rhythm on my chest.

Then I snatched the sheets away. Her skin was honey-colored in the morning light. I was still a solid member of *Saber Tooth* at this point and our next gig was three hours away.

The van would wait.

I started sending Sara vintage post cards from the road – *See Rock City!* – with a two-word phrase scrawled on the back, like "Surrender, Dorothy," or "Knock Knock," or "Zoom Zoom!"

I'd sign it with the big cursive "S" I've been perfecting for when we start doing autographs.

So sure, when I knock-knock, she lets me in, all giggly that I'm standing there. But I know that won't last. Girls look at you differently when you're between bands.

When we met, I was part of *Saber Tooth*.

Now, I'm just a fluffy-haired waif with a vintage Farfisa organ, a 400-watt Fender amp, and $45 in cash.

Not counting the time we were asleep, Sara and I had only spent four hours with each other and most of that was in the dark. Now I saw that Sara was one of those in-between girls – not pretty, not plain – somewhere in between. I hadn't noticed how she was always pushing her limp hair behind her ears. Or how a small constellation of leftover teenage zits lingered along her jaw.

But seeing her smiling in the doorway that day felt like someone had thrown me a lifeline.

It didn't take long to tumble into her squeaky iron bed. Sara had a drama degree from USF and, as we curled up afterward, she told she had just played a lunatic in what must have been a very stinky production called *Marat/Sade* directed by some semi-famous visiting actor from England named Lynn Whitehall.

"To get the authentic feel of an asylum in 1808, Lynn didn't let us wash our costumes the entire run. After the first week, the whole theater smelled like a wet gym shoe. It was incredible!"

I watched from her bed as Sara pulled on a T-shirt and jeans.

"I've got an audition downtown today. Wanna come?"

***

The audition was at a 1920s theater called The Falk. The Tampa Jewel Players, named after a cheap cigar made in Ybor, were moving up after the stinky success of *Marat/Sade* – renting a big theater for a full production of the musical, *Cabaret*.

As we pushed through the double doors off the street, a pudgy girl with a frizz of hair and very thick glasses smiled at Sara, scratched something on her notepad, and sent her through the lobby toward a hand-lettered sign saying "WOMEN. "

She looked eagerly at me.

"Name?"

"No, I'm just here…"

"For the audition, I know. We're a little short of men, so I'm really happy you're here. Name?"

"Salvo."

"Excuse me?

"Salvo."

Her smile faded a bit.

"Like the dishwashing detergent?" she asked.

Salvo – and all the names in *Saber Tooth* – had appeared as if by magic on a night when a club paid us in tequila. I didn't know much, but I was sure Bruce Jones wasn't a proper New Wave moniker. Salvo - now that was a name with some power. I guess some detergent executive thought so too.

"It's a stage name," I told her.

"Love it," she said, scratching more notes on her pad. "Go this way."

In no time, I was standing alone on a bare stage in a single pink spotlight. I knew there were seats in front of me, but all I could see were two red EXIT signs floating in the darkness.

From somewhere out front a high tenor voice shouted, "Sing!"

I opened my mouth, planning to offer up a verse or two of *Zoom My Heart*, but instead out came something my mother used to sing while vacuuming our house in Parma Heights.

I looked down and my fingers were snapping out a swing beat.

"Pack up all my cares and woe, here I go, singing low. Bye, Bye Blackbird…"

"Thanks, mate," shouted the high tenor voice, this time with a distinct British accent.

I almost skipped into the darkened wings, exhilarated by the song and the place – an actual theater with a wide wooden stage and an array of lights hanging from gridwork above, not a carpeted platform jammed in the corner of a concrete block bar reeking of cigarettes and yesterday's beer.

Out of the shadows, a woman appeared. She was Greek or Persian or some combination of Mediterranean curves and curls with skin like a china plate. She moved very close. All I could see were oval gray eyes and a regal nose. She pressed the tips of her fingers on each side of my temple.

"Salvo, I'm Camille. You're not nervous, are you?"

Pressing her fingers into my temples, she turned my head left, then right as we both mouthed "No."

"Good. Just relax. Would you like to be in this show with me, Salvo?"

She moved my head up and down so I'm nodding as we both mouthed "Yes."

"Good."

Camille released my head and looked me up and down – like a butcher checking out a side of beef.

"So you and Sara?"

"Yeah...I guess..."

Camille smiled and slapped me gently on the cheek.

"You'll do just fine," she said, before she slipped back into the shadows.

That night, I was sitting at the kitchen table watching Sara open a bottle of wine, when the phone rang. Sara listened for a moment then held the phone in my direction.

"They want you," she said.

***

Rehearsal began on The Falk stage under a white wash of light.

Twenty-five actors and singers gathered around Lynn Whitehall, our rag doll of a director, and the owner of the British accent I had heard at the auditions. Somehow from moment to moment he managed to be mannish and girlish, young and not young, friendly and not friendly. He had the jittery limbs and clinched eyes of a speed freak, though his drugs of choice were caffeine from a never-empty cup of coffee, and nicotine from the cigarettes he sucked up during rehearsal breaks like a kid inhaling a milkshake through a straw.

For some rehearsals, he arrived in khaki slacks and a blue cotton dress shirt, pocked with cigarette burns. Other nights, he was in a paisley caftan that brushed the top of sandals Jesus might have worn. His shoe-polish black hair hung, Prince Valiant-like, to his chin.

No matter his outfit or his mood, his opening lines – delivered after a sharp clap of his hands and intoned in a German accent – were always the same:

"Meine Dammen und Herren, velcome to ze Kit Kat Klub. In heah life iz beautiful. Our girls are beautiful. Our boys are beautiful. Inside these walls, everything und everyone iz desperately, dangerously, orgasmically beautiful. All I ask iz that vhen you come heah, you leaf your troubles outside. Can you do that? Can you? Say YES!"

We all barked "YES!"

"Alright then," he shouted, back in his English voice. "Now let all those bloody American inhibitions goooooooooo!"

Where *Saber Tooth* started each show by gathering in the van for a ceremonial bong hit, the Tampa Jewel Players circled up for 20-minutes of theatrical calisthenics, moves that would look natural in the monkey house at the zoo.

Lynn raised his arms, wiggled his fingers, contorted his face and 25 eager young people followed suit. We juked and jiggled. We dropped to the floor and writhed. We jogged in circles. As we trotted around, our master barked out odd names and we gave them back in what sounded more like sneezes than words: "Camus!" "Sartre!"

"Chekhov!!!"

It was crazy but the view was great. There were 9 men and 16 women on stage and the women wriggled about in leotards, midriff-bearing t-shirts, and ballet slippers, hair pulled back in scrunchies – like extras from last year's big movie *Flash Dance*.

The warm-up finished with 25 bodies in a circle on the floor like points on a compass. Lynn, also on the floor, found a lower register and recited mantra-like: "Give us this day our daily air, let it flow in and out of us. Let it flow through us like molasses, like mercury, like miracles, like magic, like mojo, like chariots swinging low, like a slow, slow night of sweet, sweet sex with somebody's ex. Amen!"

"Amen," we echoed.

That's when Paul Barber appeared, juggling three clubs, the kind shaped like bowling pins, a lit cigarette dangling from his lips. Sara had told me Paul and Camille were lovers who founded the Tampa Jewel Players in 1983. A publicity poster on an easel in the lobby showed the two of them wrapped together provocatively, dressed like actors in those PBS Shakespeare plays my mom made me watch. Camille held a whip, while Paul juggled three human skulls.

Paul didn't just walk, he moved like a cat stalking an oblivious bird. From my side view on the stage floor I noticed he had the pouf of hair, the narrow waist and hips, and the sharp facial features that reminded me of…well…me.

Paul eased around the circle of panting players – the clubs spinning and dropping into his hands, then spinning again - until he was standing over me, his feet pointed toward the top of my head. He looked down briefly, then back to his juggling. Looking up all I saw were three silver and black bowling pins floating over my head. A teardrop of ashes from his untended cigarette drifted down onto my cheek.

"So you're Salvo. The understudy," he finally said. "Can you act?"

A week earlier, I'd gotten a copy of the script and the music from Donna, the chubby girl who was the stage manager. She told me I was a sailor with three lines and a lot of backup singing parts, and maybe one other minor thing.

"What's an understudy?" I asked Paul.

"Don't worry about it. I'm like the fuckin' post office – rain, snow, sleet, hangovers – I never miss a show."

***

I should mention here that in the month after I got cast and she didn't Sara and I evolved from snuggly lovers into carnival bumper cars colliding around her suddenly tiny apartment.

It didn't help that I was broke. I had pawned my amp and sold a couple of liters of blood plasma – something the whole band had done a few times to keep us alive on the road.

The morning after the first rehearsal, I woke late to find Sara's side of the bed empty. On her pillow was a vintage post card, that famous image of *The Hindenburg* going up in flames.

On the back she had written two words: "Out! Out!" She signed it with a big cursive S that she had clearly copied from me.

Note to self, dating smart girls always comes back to bite you on the ass.

The only number I had for anyone else in Tampa was Donna, the smiling stage manager. Later that day, a very cranky version of Donna showed me my new home, a tiny dressing room up in the belfry of The Falk.

The wings of the old theater went up four stories. Rusted metal stairs switch-backed along the east and west walls, stopping at a series of tiny dressing rooms. Mine was at the top – seven flights up and without a front door.

Sweating and gulping air after the long climb, Donna silently waved me in. I saw a single wooden chair and a bare mattress, the fabric splotched with gray stains I didn't want to identify. A cloudy mirror and a wooden shelf hung from one wall. The bathroom did have a door, but the sink had been knocked off the wall and sat cracked and rusting in the corner. The pull-chain toilet was missing the seat.

"Now this is important," Donna told me as she handed me a large silver key that opened the stage door. "There's only one guard and he's usually in the front office from 3 to 11 and always drunk. As far as he's concerned, you don't live here. Right?"

Years of sneaking showers at RV parks and getting dressed in the bombed-out bathrooms of dingy nightclubs had prepared me for my new home.

"That'll work," I said. "Thanks a lot."

"Don't thank me. Lynn and I are against this. But Camille insisted."

***

That first night, the cast spent three hours around a piano singing through the score, and doing some work on vocal parts, as Lynn and Donna listened.

Before we broke for the night, Lynn coupled up the dancers, singers and other minor characters. He told us the first three rows of the theater would be removed and some of the audience - and all of us - would sit at cabaret tables during the nightclub scenes.

"And I don't want sitting. I want nuzzling. I want groping. I want lips on necks, on ears, on cleavage and on anyplace else you can think of. We're stopping short of penetration, but up to that point, you're free to improvise."

That was not going to be difficult. My lap partner was one of the Kit Kat Girls that I'd been noticing. Barbara Carley was tiny, but had a body that tested the stretchability of her lycra leotard in all the right places. She had the blue eyes and upturned nose of a high school cheerleader. Her hair was all scrambled up in tiny curls. When she slid onto my lap, she felt light as a child and smelled of Dr. Bonner's organic soap.

"Work, work, work," she said, extending her hand. "I'm Barbara."

"Salvo."

She cocked her head, her tawny-colored eyes going even wider.

"It's a stage name," I said.

Over the next few minutes we got the preliminaries out of the way.

I told her about my forced departure from *Saber Tooth*.

She told me she was a drama major at USF, but I was relieved to learn that Sara had graduated before she arrived. I also found out she was Camille's understudy, which didn't mean much, since Camille, like Paul, apparently never missed a show.

"I think I've got Sally's part down," she said. "So are you off-book?"

"Which book?"

"Ohhh, this is going to be interesting. You know anything about Lynn?"

I remembered what Sara had told me about the unwashed costumes from the insane asylum play.

"All I know is that in one show he wants it stinky and in the next he wants it sexy. I'm glad I'm in the sexy show. What's he doing here?"

"Word is he's here laying low for a while. He was doing some big movies in London when the tabloids outed him for some all-male orgy while he was at RADA."

99

I gave her a quizzical look.

"Royal Academy of Dramatic Arts? Never mind. It's big. Anyway, we're lucky to have him but I've got three words of advice – learn your dialogue – even if you never have to use it."

Just then, Paul Barber appeared again, sliding his hand slowly across Barbara's shoulders. He leaned in and whispered something in her ear.

When Barbara turned back, she was blushing.

"You and Paul?" I asked, hoping I was mistaken about what I was seeing.

She tilted her head to the left, her face set in a comic grimace.

There was a Greek diner on the corner near The Falk, and Barbara joined me there after the rehearsal. She sipped herb tea while I washed down scrambled eggs and hash browns with four cups of scalding black coffee.

"I'm calling him my college mistake. You're supposed to have one, right? So Paul's mine. He taught a master-class in stage combat. After he threw me to the mat and fell on top of me, he whispered in that radio announcer voice: 'Let's make love, not war.' That was it, I guess."

"But there's Camille…"

"Oh, there's always Camille," she laughed. "I think Paul's only happy when he's juggling."

"Yeah, the frickin' juggling. What's up with that?"

"He did a couple of years on the Renaissance Fair circuit. Says he's staying in practice in case things here don't work out."

"Things with you?"

"Paul has a lot of things," she said.

The traffic on Kennedy Boulevard had eased as midnight approached and we walked back to Barbara's car through a misting rain. We didn't talk, but it was an easy silence, like the end of a perfect first date.

Barbara drove a tiny, red Honda Civic. She put the key in the door, then looked back at me and smiled. In the glow of the streetlights, the tiny droplets of rain in her curls shimmered like diamonds.

"Salvo. I'll get used to that. Anyway, thanks for the tea and the talk."

She stood on tiptoes and kissed my cheek. As she drove away, I watched until her taillights disappeared into the night.

***

After our second rehearsal, I emptied a newspaper rack outside the theater and carried the papers up the seven flights to the top of the belfry. It was a life-threatening climb along those shaky stairs in the dim glow of a single bare bulb atop a standing lamp - what I learned later was The Ghost Light, required by theater tradition to burn all night on the empty stage.

Working in almost complete darkness, I managed to spread the newspaper sections over the mattress. A cushion lifted from a chair in the lobby was my pillow. It wasn't great, but when you've spent weeks in a sleeping bag on the floor of an Econoline van, an actual mattress inside a dry building was a big step up.

One thing I learned about being in a touring band that was constantly broke: when you are asleep, you don't spend money. So doing 12, 15 hours at a stretch was fine with me. After the first eight hours, the dreams get really vivid.

That morning was no exception: I was a superhero, able to leap into the air and fly, but I couldn't get more than two or three feet above the ground. I kept willing myself higher, but I couldn't climb. This was a problem since I was flying really fast and kept running into benches and trees and cars and...

"Salvo!"

I woke to find Camille standing on the landing outside my room, holding some sheets and an actual bed pillow.

"Poor baby," Camille said, dropping the sheets and pillow on the table, then leaning down so her breasts, barely tucked inside a V-necked T-shirt and unbound by any Playtex products, completely filled my field of vision. "I thought you might need some things."

She sat down on the edge of the mattress and offered up a very sexy smile - her face round and pale, wrapped by a cloak of wavy black curls. She reached out with red-tipped fingers and tousled my hair.

"So Hermia has exiled her poor Lysander to the enchanted forest?"

"What?"

"Sara tossed you out?"

"You know, we kind of grew apart..." I said, sitting up.

"Camille!" It was Paul calling from somewhere below.

"Up here, with Salvo, in the attic!" She shouted, her fingers gently massaging my scalp as Paul's boots clanked up the metal stairs.

"We got some Sally and Cliff scenes to run," he said from the landing.
The butt of a cigarette smoldered in his lips and three bean bags floated from his hands into the air. He wore his usual rehearsal uniform – black jeans, white T-shirt and Doc Martin boots. I thought it would be a good outfit for my next band, which I had decided should be more *The Clash* and less *The Cars*.

102

"I'll be right down," Camille said a bit too sweetly. "Had to make sure our understudy had everything he might need... or want."

Camille slid her palm down my cheek, my neck, along my chest and stopped, her fingers extended, just above my crotch. I stared down, just to make sure what I was feeling was actually happening.

"I think he's okay," Paul said, his fiery gaze focused on the progress of Camille's wandering digits. The three unwatched bean bags took turns falling to the landing with a marshmallow thud.

"I agree," said Camille. "I think he's fine."

When I looked back at Paul, he was eyeing me like some kind of madman. If this had been *Star Trek*, Paul's eyes would have been set on "*Stun*." He held me there for a long beat, then tossed his cigarette butt to the ground, stamping it out with a black boot. He left the bean bags where they fell.

"Five minutes," he hollered over his shoulder as he pounded down the stairs.

Camille looked back at me, a spike of pain flashing across her face like the first lightning bolt from an approaching storm.

"You okay?" I asked.

"Take my word for it, Salvo, love is a many splintered thing."

The storm passed and her sexy smile returned. Her fingers slid across my crotch and down to my thigh. She sank her hand into the meaty part of my leg, as she straightened her arm and pushed herself upright until she was towering over me like an Amazon goddess.

"Let me know if you need anything else from me," she whispered, her voice almost purring. She turned slowly. At the landing she knelt and gathered the three bean bags, sticking them in her pocket. She looked back over her shoulder at me, then disappeared down the stairs.

***

There are a lot of things I do well. I could play *Fur Elise* better than any of the other kids at Mrs. Taylor's piano recital – even the girls. I could always find a high harmony on the first try. And when Speeze launched into a hot guitar solo, I always knew just the right combination of chords and rhythm to put underneath.

But memorizing a script full of dialogue was apparently not in my repertoire. In this production of *Cabaret*, Camille is Sally Bowles, Lynn the MC and Paul is Cliff, Sally's love interest, and he has page after page of things to say.

I ran lines with Donna at the end of each rehearsal but except for Cliff's recitation of *Casey At the Bat* when he first meets Sally, I couldn't manage to remember much once I put the book down.

***

It was 10 p.m. about a week into the rehearsals. Donna and I were in the wings, running lines. Or she's reading lines and I'm coming up blank. Lynn appeared like some phantom transvestite in his paisley caftan just as Donna hurled her script to the ground in disgust.

"I don't think he can do it," she said.

"Maybe I shouldn't have smoked so much dope in high school," I quipped, trying to lighten the situation.

I mean, I'm just the understudy, right?

Lynn stomped over and stuck his face in mine, those caffeinated eyes laced with red lightning bolts.

"You're doing shit work, mate! Shit work! I didn't think we should cast some stoned-out rock 'n roller, and you are proving me right."

I was hoping I could sink into the wooden chair when Barbara appeared, resting her hand on Lynn's shoulder.

"I've had a lot of luck getting folks off-book," Barbara said, her voice soothing and confident.

I felt better just listening to her.

"Give me a week and he'll be good to go."

Lynn gave her a hard look, then leaned back into my face. He had turned down the crazy about two notches.

"Last chance, mate. Don't blow it."

The caftan whirled off into the wings as Barbara reached out her hand.

"Salvo, let's get some coffee."

***

The early days in a new band are like being in the family you always wanted. Things click. You're sharing your life with a bunch of guys who get your jokes. But down the road a few weeks or months, and it's like you're trapped in a foster family of psychos.

I learned quickly that doing theater is the same, minus the long drives.

As low man on the totem pole, I mostly ignored the slammed dressing room doors, the huddled whispering between Lynn and Donna, and the angry eruptions whenever Camille and Paul were together.

What I looked forward to was 10 p.m. when rehearsal ended and I'd sit across from Barbara at the diner or in the bucket seats of her tiny Honda working over Cliff and Sally's dialogue.

Call me shallow, but I do better work with cute girls. As opening night approached, Barbara got me off-book, as promised.

First she had me running the lines in some call-and-response gospel style, then we were singing the words, like lyrics, and somewhere in there, they stuck. And doing the scenes with Barbara, it didn't feel like acting. Due to complications beyond our control, Barbara and I weren't allowed to fall in love, but during those hours, we could pretend we were Sally and Cliff, trying to sort out a complicated romance in a Berlin apartment:

CLIFF

"Maybe I like you here. I need you. The truth is – when you are out all night – I can't sleep. Our little bed seems so empty…I've never felt this way before about – anyone – anyone at all."

SALLY

"You truly mean this?"

CLIFF

"More than I've ever meant anything."

SALLY

"Oh, darling…"

But then, after about an hour, Paul would appear – blowing the horn in his vintage Mustang from the diner parking lot. Or tapping on the window of the Honda, cigarette dangling. He'd sneer at me, then walk away.

Sally Bowles would turn back into Barbara Carley. She'd cock her head and give me that "what's a girl to do?" grimace.

Then she'd go chasing after him.

And I'd return to the theater, slipping quietly into the stage door, and there was Camille, perched on a stool beside the ghost light, reading her script. And every night, I'd step into that circle of light and wait.

Camille would eventually close her script, climb off the stool and walk into the shadowy wings toward the stairs.

Like a puppy, I'd follow.

***

The final dress rehearsal did not go well.

I mean, the first few songs were fine, Lynn was so eerily good as the MC, I was thinking maybe I should try to build a band around him. And Barbara, playing a Kit Kat Girl in leather and black lace, was right up there with him.

But the Sally and Cliff scenes – the main love story that supported the entire musical – were more like a televised boxing match.

Camille and Paul spit lines at each other. A kiss would break with almost a shove.

That tension began to spill over to the other actors, who dropped lines, and to the dancers, who got tangled during numbers they previously had down. Even the band, which had nailed the show during the rehearsals, sounded off key. The young tenor singing lead on the choral number, *Tomorrow Belongs To Me*, forgot to come back in with his solo line and I had to sing his part or we would have been standing there all night.

Lynn was waiting when I came offstage. He actually clapped me on the back and smiled.

"Good instincts, mate."

Toward the end though, Lynn's smile was gone. The show didn't feel like two acts. More like 15 long, bloody rounds.

When the dress rehearsal was over, Lynn, still in his MC's tux and white-face makeup, gathered the four of us – his two stars and their understudies - on the stage. He told Donna to send everyone else home.

Camille sat on a stool by the ghost light, Lynn and Donna were nearby whispering anxiously to each other. Barbara and I hung back a bit, just out of the circle of light, hoping they'd forget we were there.

Finally, Paul appeared from the wings, still dressed in Cliff's 1930s suit, his feet bare. It was a scary sight. He was juggling a sickle, a hatchet, and a long-handled switchblade. All three blades looked seriously sharp in the stage lights.

"We can't put *THAT* on stage tomorrow night," Lynn announced. "Donna and I have talked. We're going with the understudies until you two work out whatever is going on here."

I looked at Camille sitting on the stool. The Amazon princess had drained away. She looked like a sad young girl, fighting back tears.

"Maybe Lynn is right. I can't do this any longer," she said, her moist eyes on Paul.

"That's utter bullshit," Paul said, moving slowly, the three blades spinning, toward Barbara and me. His face was blood red. His eyes slits, focused only on the rotating blades in front of him.

"You'd put this punk on stage instead of me? Sorry, not while this theater company has my name on the letterhead. I don't care what Camille says. Look at him, he's not an actor, he's a fuckin' disgrace…"

I felt my face reddening too. And my eyes narrowing, just like Paul's. From somewhere down in my gut, anger was rising. Anger about everything - Sara, Speeze, Camille, *Saber Tooth*, and now this pompous asshole.

Right then, Paul and I must have looked like twins ready to launch into a joint tantrum.

"Paul, take it easy, okay?" It was Barbara, stepping slowly toward him.

"Did I ask you to speak?" he shouted, eyes still on his juggling. "Until I do, just shut the fuck up!"

It's hard to explain what happened next.

Everything around me went red and all I could see was Paul's sneering face. I stepped obliviously into the rotation of the blades and threw my very first ever roundhouse punch – my fist catching fire as it slammed into his jaw.

Paul's head jerked but he didn't fall. Instead, his eyes widened and his right hand pressed against his jaw.

The ax and the sickle clattered to the floor around us. The switchblade spun at the top of the arc, then, in slow motion, dove blade-first for the stage, sinking itself up to the hilt in Paul's right foot.

***

So here I am. The understudy on opening night before a full house, playing Cliff to Camille's Sally.

In the play, when Sally and Cliff meet in Berlin, she is so happy to hear someone speaking English she begs Cliff - "Keep talking, please!"

So he does – reciting *Casey At The Bat*.

No problem.

"Somewhere in this favored land the sun is shining bright. A band is playing somewhere and somewhere hearts are light. And somewhere men are laughing and somewhere children shout. But there is no joy in Mudville, mighty Casey has struck out!"

Sally smiles that smile, the one that cripples me.

"Oh yes," she says. "Please don't stop."

And I don't want to stop, but when I reopen the notebook in my mind, I find a blank, unlined page. All I can recall is the moment after the punch, Paul nailed to the floor, blood running down his chin and spurting, geyser-like, from his foot. Camille on her knees, her arms wrapped around his legs, screaming for help.

Now, less than 24 hours later, she's looking desperately around the stage for help again.

"Salvo, you can do this!" she whispers sharply in my ear.

But I can't, and I feel Camille holding me up as my knees give way.

Then, from stage left, comes a deep, radio-announcer's voice:

"Somewhere in this favored land the sun is shining bright. A band is playing somewhere and somewhere hearts are light. And somewhere men are laughing and somewhere children shout. But there is no joy in Mudville, mighty Casey has struck out!"

Paul, still in his bloody suit, a Tiny-Tim crutch under one arm, is limping toward us.

Camille lets me go and I sink to the stage. I feel someone lifting me and when I look up I see Barbara. She keeps whispering "It's okay," like a mother comforting a crying child. Soon I'm in her lap at a cabaret table, her arms tight around my waist.

When I look back at the stage, I see Camille walking slowly toward Paul as they trade Sally and Cliff 's lines. When she gets close, they stand face to face for a long beat, not speaking. Slowly, Camille leans in and kisses Paul on the lips. His arm comes around behind her, a hand going to the center of her back. He pulls her even closer.

It is Berlin in 1933 and Sally and Cliff are clearly in love.

110

Applause bursts from the audience at the kiss, spinning my head in that direction.

All I can see, floating in the darkness at the back of the theater are two glowing signs and just then I realize I've found the perfect name for my new band:

EXIT! EXIT!

THE APPRENTICE

Looking down at the chicken boiling in the stock pot, Katrina thought it could be Brian - if she had tweezed out all his hair and let his severed head soak overnight. The violet Rorschach splotch visible just below the bird's waxy-white skin was where she cracked his brittle skull with the hardcover edition of *The Collected Poems of William Butler Yeats*, ending his shallow, privileged life.

I didn't smack him. I smote him.

I *visited him disastrously.*

I *struck him with passion and emotion.*

Smite. Smote. Smitten.

It was Biblical!

After four years of poetry workshops Katrina couldn't help herself. And almost eight months after picking up her BFA, definitions and synonyms still ticked through her brain like playing cards snapping against the spokes of a bike tire.

And she could turn almost anything into a symbol or a metaphor.

The boiling bird represented the death of her love affair but the diced tomatoes, celery and bell peppers floating alongside, their Crayola colors vivid, were the new life she was cooking up from the old.

"Ola, Katrina! Despierta mi pequeña soñadora! Wake up! Time to skim. Skim!"

Katrina snapped back from her revenge reverie and saw Maria miming a skimming motion with her cupped hand, the tips of her stubby fingers golden from dredging trout filets through flour, egg and spices.

Trout a la Rusa was the day's special at La Septima Café.

Maria enjoyed it when she caught Katrina disappearing inside her head. After the first few times, she had dubbed her kitchen apprentice *Mi Pequeña Soñadora,* "my little dreamer. "

Katrina picked up the big spoon and began to skim off the mucus-colored bubbles of fat rising to the surface of the pot.

So much for poetic justice, Katrina thought, as she skimmed.

Brian was alive and probably driving a new girlfriend around the Detroit suburbs in his black BMW while the chicken boiling in Ybor City would soon be deboned and spooned into a pan of rice yellowed with saffron and turmeric.

Deboned.

There was a word waiting for a poem.

Brian, I de-bone you. I de-lete you. I de-stroy you

But there were no new poems.

Since the day she had awakened and found Brian's goodbye note on her writing desk, along with a small stack of twenty-dollar bills, Katrina believed her muse had left town with him. She refused to write any sad love poems. She'd heard too many delivered by sensitive sophomores who turned a break up with a horny frat boy into some very painful poetry:

Porcelain pillow
blue veins drain
love's red remains
going south
down a corrugated river

Not that Brian was a college fling or horny frat boy.

Together most of their senior year at the University of Michigan, they had taken a post-graduate road trip to the writerly Southern towns of Oxford and New Orleans. As August gave way to September, they found themselves in a rent-by-the- week apartment in Ybor City.

Katrina imagined them as the Hemingways slumming in Paris. She loved the aging authenticity of the historic district, the poetry scene around the Three Birds Bookstore, and the exotic food, a mix of Spanish, Cuban and Italian dishes that had arrived with the immigrants who built Ybor at the turn of the 20th century.

Part of her had always known Brian wasn't a forever thing, no matter how many promises he whispered while they made love. He talked about becoming a writer, but the only thing he wrote were random entries in a journal he left open on the kitchen table:

October 12, 1985: Warm and windy today. Washed the car. Out of dental floss.

A finance major, he confessed he had come to her weekly poetry group thinking it would be a good place to meet girls.

"Will you dump me if I admit I didn't get that poem you read?" he asked her, on the first night they spent at his off-campus apartment, a luxury two-bedroom he had all to himself.

"Will you dump me if I admit I don't really understand men?"

"Don't worry. I'm not that complicated," Brian replied.

She should have taken that as a warning. Instead, Katrina snuggled into him on sheets as crisp as fine parchment. He was tall and funny and he smelled like a walk in the morning through an evergreen forest.

Katrina realized now that she was his gap year. His artsy experiment. He was always headed back to Bloomfield Hills where his father was a battery magnate. Or was it solenoids?

And Katrina was always going to be the daughter of a union carpenter and a high school guidance counselor from Flint. The academic scholarships, the poems and short stories published in obscure literary magazines couldn't change those facts.

Brian had said as much in a note that was barely longer than his journal entries:

It's not you. It's not me. It's the "us" that's broken.

He added a shaky metaphor about two planets with briefly overlapping orbits or some crap like that.

After she tore Brian's note into tiny pieces and flushed them down the toilet, Katrina let the shower pound her until the hot water ran out. Then she stood naked in front a mirror, noticing a thickness in her hips, a heaviness in her breasts she had never seen before.

If she had written about herself before the breakup, Katrina would have used a word like "willowy": *tall, slim, slender, svelte, lissome, long-limbed, graceful.*

She wouldn't use the word "beautiful": *attractive, pretty, alluring.*

Her features were too sharp, her lips too thin for that. But she was long-legged and lean with a high-wattage smile and dark Joan Baez hair she let fall below her shoulders or wrapped in a loose knot around a single chopstick. She looked like a girl you might spot across the room at a smoky party in an artist's loft.

Katrina still fit into her college uniform - vintage cotton dresses with flowing skirts and a sexy scoop at the neck, but the clothes were tighter. The road trip, the hours in bed, the long lunches and dinners, the sheer happiness she had felt with Brian had settled itself on her body.

What was added by love is now weighing me down.

There was a poem there somewhere.

Her college girlfriends swore by "The Heartbreak Diet," that sick-to-your-stomach ache guaranteed to drop all the happiness weight you picked up during a love affair. But after tossing in bed each night, her thoughts shifting from revenge to remorse, Katrina woke up ravenous.

Instead of paying her rent or buying a ticket home with the money Brian had left, she used it to eat her way through Ybor: *Boliche*, from the Colombia Restaurant; *Crab Chilau*, at the Seabreeze; and *Picadillo*, a fragrant Cuban stew of ground beef and tomatoes, with raisins for sweetness and olives for salt, from La Septima Café.

Katrina was savoring that dish when she met Santiago.

"I like a woman with a good appetite."

The man standing over her corner table was tall and swarthy, with the thick curly hair of a teenager, but the fleshy look of a middle-aged man who had never missed a meal. His girth was partly camouflaged by a white guayabera, the loose-fitting Cuban dress shirts, with four front pockets, favored by Ybor businessmen of a certain age.

Katrina could smell mint after-shave and thought she saw makeup covering the craggy remains of teen-age acne.

"I am Santiago," he said, his manicured, feminine hand settling on her shoulder. "I like to make up stories about my customers. It passes the time. Want to hear what I came up with for you?"

"I like a good story," Katrina said, shifting a little, hoping he would get the hint and remove his hand.

"You are a beautiful young heiress from Manhattan on the run from a domineering father. You are hiding out in Ybor City pretending to be an artist, but secretly hoping you'll meet the love of your life. How's that?"

"You could tell all that just by looking at me?"

"It's a gift."

Katrina smiled up at Santiago like a teenage girl who had just been asked to the prom by the best-looking guy at school.

"I'm not looking for love, but I am looking for a waitress job. Any chance I could work here...for you?"

"You've waited tables before?"

"All through school," Katrina lied.

Aside from keeping the house and making dinners for her dad and her younger brother after her mom died, Katrina's work experience was wrapping Christmas presents each December at J.C. Penney.

But she wasn't ready to go home. She needed to eat and pay the rent on her apartment, a light-filled one-bedroom above an art gallery on Seventh Avenue. And these exotic Ybor dishes – so different from any of her Midwestern meals - gave her the only joy she'd felt since Brian left.

Santiago told her to come back the next morning and wear black.

"If I could, I'd really love to learn how you make this," she said, lifting her half-empty plate.

"I can teach you many things," he said, his hand sliding slowly down her arm.

***

Florida is normally dry in October but 1985 was different. To Katrina the dense charcoal clouds and daylong downpours that arrived the same week Brian left were simply the world bending to her mood.

But as she walked to work her first day, the sky was crystal blue and cloudless, the air cool and lifted on a soft breeze.

Turning slowly in circles to take in the day, as words and images danced in her head, Katrina didn't notice she had drifted off the sidewalk and into the still-quiet street.

If Ybor City hadn't existed, she thought, Tennessee Williams might have conjured it. The old world downtown, barely a mile from Tampa's "American" downtown, was a red brick and wrought iron *Belle Reve*, clinging desperately to a gilded past, while fraying at the edges.

She thought of Santiago, a man she didn't know, offering her a job.

"I have always depended on the kindness…"

A lone car, cruising slowly up Seventh, honked and Katrina leapt quickly onto the hexagonal block sidewalk.

Just after eight, she pushed open the heavy wooden door of La Septima Café, which took its name from the Spanish translation of Seventh Avenue. The place had plenty of *Belle Reve* about it Katrina thought.

Silver shafts of light, slicing through floor-to-ceiling windows, made the room shimmer like the inside of an antique jewelry box. Katrina saw windows framed in carved wood; a fresco of a pastoral Spanish village on the plaster ceiling; and marble floors in a grey and black geometric pattern that could have been lifted from an Escher lithograph.

The morning light also revealed jagged craters in the window frames where termites had dined; the fresco was faded, like a tattoo on an aging sailor; the floor bore the scuffs of a hundred thousand footfalls.

The word that clicked into her mind was "evanescence": *to slowly fade out of sight, memory, or existence.*

The restaurant was empty, wooden café chairs stacked upside down on the tables, but a harsh fluorescent glare spilled from an open door in back.

The door led into a narrow galley kitchen where a middle-aged woman was working under the buzz of a fluorescent fixture. Metal countertops ran along both walls, and an old gas stove, heavy as a floor safe, sat at the end, its white porcelain exterior stained yellow. Burners were lit under a stockpot and a large frying pan filled the room with the nutty aroma of sautéed garlic and olive oil. A single strand of hot mist escaped from the corner of the oven, rising like campfire smoke toward the pressed tin ceiling.

Katrina's mind clicked through adjectives to describe the room: steaming, stifling, suffocating.

Yes, suffocating: *to feel or cause to feel trapped and oppressed.*

The woman at the counter was muscling a carving knife through a fat onion, her simple cotton dress soaked in sweat. Like the stove behind her, the woman was squat and solid. Her dress and stained apron could have been wrapping a block of wood.

She was quietly crying.

"Are you okay?" Katrina asked.

Startled, the woman turned suddenly, wiping away some tears with the back of her hand. She didn't speak, only glared at Katrina, her hair hidden inside a black net, her narrow lips pressed together.

"I'm Katrina. The new waitress? Santiago told me to be here at 10 but I wanted to come early. He told me......"

"My husband says a lot of things," she said, her words coming out cold and deliberate.

"Your husband?"

"He also doesn't say a lot of things."

The woman's face didn't soften. Instead, she turned back to her chopping, the flesh of the onion giving way to her silver blade with a moist "KA-CHUNK."

"Are you the chef? Your food...I mean, I wanted to work here because I fell in love with your food. I've never tasted anything like it."

The woman turned back, fresh onion tears ringing her eyes.

"I'm a cook. Not a chef."

Katrina flashed her best Midwestern smile.

"I'd love to know how you do what you do. If you'd teach me."

"So you can steal *mi esposo* and take over my job?"

Four years of high school Spanish had been helpful since Katrina had moved to this place.

"I wouldn't do either of those things," Katrina said. "Besides, I've sworn off men,"

"*Por que?*"

"I don't know…they are…beyond my control. I don't like that."

The woman stared for a long moment at Katrina. Her face slowly unclenched and she almost chuckled.

She picked up a large onion and held it out in her palm.

"*Este cebolla* is like a man. Thin skin. He thinks he's deep, but each layer is just like the one before. And he will make you cry – *absolutamente!*"

She held up the big knife.

"*Mi nombre es Maria. Y tu?*

"Katrina."

"So Katrina, want to chop up a few men?"

"Oh yes, please!"

***

What Katrina didn't know about waiting tables was a lot.

Santiago arrived 10 minutes before the restaurant opened at 11 with a zippered bag stuffed with cash for the register and offered no lessons beyond suggesting she open the top three buttons of her blouse.

"Customers like a little peek when you lean in," he whispered, his hand now firmly in the center of her back.

He flashed a toothy, knowing smile, like he had just shared a great secret of life, then he walked to the high wooden table by the front door that held the cash register, a press-box of wooden toothpicks, a smoked glass bowl of mints and a jelly jar filled with plastic pens. Santiago settled himself onto a tall stool, a spot he left only when an attractive woman appeared at one of his tables.

Carmen, a bone-thin woman Maria introduced as her cousin, arrived at 10 to prep the dining room. Katrina guessed Carmen could be anywhere from 25 to 55. Her precise little face was masked in pale peach foundation, her eyes racooned with ebony eyeliner and dandruff-sized specks of mascara. Her reddish hair was teased and sprayed into a helmet that could have topped a Roman Centurion.

Carmen checked her look in a small, gold-plated compact, her index finger – dabbed in red – moved slowly around the edges of her lips, as she explained the rules of the restaurant to the new girl.

"I get the first two tables of the day and all the tables along the windows. You get the rest. OK?"

"Anything else I should know?"

"Don't drop a tray. Santiago hates that, he takes the loss out of your pay. Or he suggests another payment plan. Either way, it's not good."

***

Katrina didn't drop a tray her first week, but she made plenty of mistakes. It helped that she smiled a lot and apologized sincerely.

Leaning in with her three top buttons undone helped too. The extra weight that had tightened her clothes, had also given her something she'd never had before – cleavage.

Maria looked at her first orders, written expansively in very precise longhand, and taught her the shortcuts, the abbreviations. The writing on her order pads quickly evolved from prose to blank verse.

But she couldn't bring herself to abbreviate the names of the dishes. To her, they sounded like music: *Frijoles Negros, Flan de Leche, Caldo Gallego, Pollo Valencia.*

By the end of the first week, Katrina had settled into a routine.

Like most Ybor restaurants, La Septima was open only for lunch. The old district was mostly deserted at night except for the 80-year-old Columbia Restaurant, a landmark at the east end of Seventh Avenue and El Goya, the busy gay bar at the west end, and the once regal Ritz Theater, now offering porn flicks to crews from the banana boats and oil tankers tied up at the Port of Tampa.

But from 11 a.m. to 2 p.m., the fifteen tables at La Septima were full with office workers from Tampa's downtown, teachers from the community college, uniformed deputies from the sheriff's substation, and a few artists who could afford to go out for lunch.

Katrina rose early each day and was waiting when Maria unlocked the big wooden door at 7 a.m. Katrina had already grabbed the brown paper bag, stuffed with a dozen loaves of fresh Cuban bread that the delivery man had left hanging outside on a nail.

They began the morning sipping steaming mugs of *café con leche*, dunking hand-torn hunks of bread, still warm from the bakery, into the milky brew.

Then came the cooking lessons. Early on, Katrina had tried to make *arroz con pollo* in the tiny kitchen of her apartment, but it didn't taste like Maria's.

"What did I do wrong?" she asked the morning after her dish had come out mushy and bland.

"You must cook everything separately. The onions, the garlic, the peppers, the chicken, the rice. Spoon them together at the last minute. The flavors need to be distinctive, not *mezclar*. *Comprende?*"

During those hours in the kitchen, Katrina told stories about growing up in Flint, her mother's fatal car accident when Katrina was fourteen, and finally, about Brian. It felt good to talk about him, even though Maria mostly nodded or said "hmmmm."

If Midwestern girls were like marigolds, wide open and holding back nothing, long-time Ybor denizens like Maria were lilies, their secrets held inside tight buds that only opened slowly with time.

What Katrina eventually learned was that the cook was an Ybor hybrid with a Cuban father and a Sicilian mother. Her family tree had branches that reached from Tampa to Miami, Madrid, Havana and the tiny Sicilian villages of Santo Stefano and Allessandra della Rocca.

She could cite the marital status and latest scandals of her first, second and third cousins.

"*Mi madre* never met anyone who wasn't a relative of some kind," Maria told her. "That's Ybor. That used to be Ybor."

Maria had learned to cook in a home where Spanish, Cuban and Italian dishes took turns on the table and your relatives lived around the corner or down the street. Now her mother was in a nursing home in North Tampa, and her relatives were spread around the area, mostly in the outlying suburbs, far from Ybor.

It took three weeks of early morning coffee and bread before Maria opened up about her marriage.

"Santiago…He was the most handsome boy at Jefferson High," she said. "His family lived two blocks away and our mothers decided we would be a good match."

Katrina could picture the mothers plotting. Santiago was vain and pampered. Maria solid and hard working. A good match.

There had been a baby long ago, a boy, but he died at three months. Then nothing.

"I'm so sorry," Katina said.

"*Así es la vida,*" she said.

When his uncle retired, Santiago took over La Septima, bringing in his wife to make magic in a hot kitchen from 7 to 3 each day. Katrina noticed the couple's exchanges were – what was the right word? – "terse": *sparing in the use of words; abrupt.*

Santiago always ended his day at 3 with a few glasses of Rioja.

During Katrina's first week, Santiago invited her each afternoon to join him for a glass. She refused, but sweetly, offering excuses about her tired feet, a class she had to get to or a sour stomach.

By the second week, Santiago stopped asking.

In truth, he had not tried very hard. Santiago's dance card was full.

In particular, there was Vivian, a substantial woman with a blond bouffant and breasts that always seemed to be escaping from the plunging necklines of her polyester dresses. She was the lone employee of the Ybor City Chamber of Commerce. Katrina liked the irony of that, since commerce had long been an endangered species in the old Latin Quarter.

Vivian lunched most days at La Septima, always with two or three men in guayaberas, or suits and ties. She laughed loudly and ate well. Her meals were always on the house, and she never left a tip. When she was in the restaurant, Santiago lingered at her table, his hand settling on Vivian's shoulder or back. His eyes taking regular hikes across her cleavage.

125

Once, when Katrina came to her table, Santiago introduced his waitress as "my *gringa*."

Vivian smiled but did not look directly at her. Instead, she lifted an empty coffee cup.

"Could I have another?"

Vivian was often the last customer to leave. Her lunch guests long departed, she and Santiago sat, leaning close and laughing loudly, over glasses of wine.

Katrina sometimes noticed Maria lingering by the kitchen door, staring at her husband and the woman. Neither of them ever looked her way.

***

Katrina continued to stop after work in Three Birds to browse the books and magazines, but she skipped the weekend poetry readings. She didn't have a telephone and she and Brian had not been in town long enough to make friends, so it was easy for her to stay home and cook.

Plus, she was tired after her shifts and she was sleeping like a teenager, sometimes ten hours at a stretch.

She told herself she was healing.

During her month at the restaurant, Katrina's sadness about Brian had faded to a dull ache, something that bothered her mostly in the middle of the night when she would wake suddenly and feel like she had forgotten to breathe.

On a Wednesday night in early November Katrina thought she had finally recreated Maria's *arroz con pollo*.

As she pulled the roasting pan from the oven, the smell put her back in Maria's kitchen. The rice was fluffy and butter yellow; the chicken khaki-colored and moist; the pimentos like vivid red buttons.

She was about to wrap up a sample to take to Maria when the first cramp bent her over.

Her roasting pan crashed to the floor, throwing rice and chicken around her bare feet.

The second cramp felt like a giant hand was squeezing everything inside her belly. It dropped Katrina to her knees. Clumps of warm rice stuck to her legs. Her cotton dress was suddenly soaked in sweat.

She couldn't decide if she was crying from the pain or because her perfect dish was now lost.

As the hand loosened its grip, Katrina managed to drag herself to the bathroom. She cramped again, and this time, she felt something rushing out of her. She heard it splash.

Katrina couldn't move for a long time. The room spun and gray dots danced in front of her eyes.

The cramps continued, but with less intensity. Like echoes deep inside her.

She finally rose and stood at the sink, letting water run into her cupped hands, then pressing her hands into her face.

She didn't want to look at the toilet, but she knew she had to look.

Her year with Brian hadn't been a dream. It was tissue and blood. It was right there.

And then, with just a touch of her hand, it was gone.

***

The morning was gray – with thunderstorms on the way - when Katrina stepped out on the sidewalk. She walked slowly, seeing the old city with new eyes: the sidewalks cracked and uneven; the paint peeling on the doors of the empty storefronts; a rusting car abandoned at an angle on a side street, one tire up on the high curb.

She longed to meet Maria at the door of La Septima and tell her everything over bread and coffee. Though it was just 7 when she arrived, the front door was unlocked and the bread gone from the hook.

Inside, the restaurant looked like it had her first day, except when she found Maria crying in the kitchen, there were no onions on the counter.

"What's wrong?" Katrina asked.

Maria just shook her head.

Katrina made coffee, fresh espresso from the Naviera roaster just down the block. She heated milk on the stove and finished the cups off with two teaspoons of sugar.

She set the steaming cup in front of Maria and waited for her to speak.

"The city is taking the building," Maria finally said, after her second sip.

"What for?"

"*No se*. What did he call it - *domain emminente?*"

"Eminent Domain. Wow. But you could move. There are lots of empty storefronts in Ybor."

Maria shook her head. She took another slow sip from the coffee.

"That woman. She is taking Santiago. *Todo ha terminado para mí.*"

Katrina went to Maria, her hands on the back of her shoulders, but

Maria shook her off.

"We must cook. I have to cook," she said.

But as she watched Maria weep over the loss of the restaurant and her marriage, Katrina felt the hand squeezing her insides. She saw the jumbled mass of tissue and blood floating in her toilet.

She leaned back against the counter, her vision narrowing as the bright kitchen dimmed.

She saw her mother's face, looking like a piece of waxed fruit, in the open casket. She saw her father in his funeral suit, his jaw set, holding her little brother, as the boy screamed and kicked, trying to break free. She saw a fourteen-year-old girl, slender, with a black ponytail, sitting in the front pew finding reasons not to cry.

A wrenching sob broke deep in Katrina's throat. She felt her nose draining and hot tears on her cheeks. The room began to spin.

Trying not to faint, Katrina bent from the waist letting blood flow to her head.

When she finally stood, Maria was holding up the carving knife and an onion and attempting a smile. For the next fifteen minutes, Katrina and Maria stood side by side, crying, as they whittled onion after onion down to tiny chunks.

Then, without speaking, they set to work on lunch, boiling chicken, prepping the trout filets, sautéing onions, garlic and peppers with fresh herbs. Boliche was the special and Maria used the meat cleaver to chop one-inch steaks from a thick tenderloin.

Each time Maria brought the blade up and swung it down it met the cutting board with a sharp CRACK! With each chop, Maria looked over at Katrina and grinned. She brought the blade up higher each time, swinging down with all her strength.

CRACK! CRACK! CRACK!

***

Santiago didn't come near the kitchen that day. When he offered Katrina a smile and a small wave, she pretended not to see it.

At 1:30, as the lunch rush slowed, Katrina spotted Vivian sitting alone at a window table. Outside, a thunderstorm was raging, but Vivian was somehow dry and looking like she'd just left the beauty shop – her hair sprayed in place, her cheeks rouged, her lips red. She wore a sleeveless emerald blue dress with a plunging neckline.

Katrina thought the tops of her breasts looked like the backs of two dolphins breaking the surface of the sea.

 Carmen refused to take the order, even though it was her table.

"Not me. Not today," she told Katrina. "You take the bitch's order and pass the plate by me so I can spit in it."

Katrina looked into the kitchen. Maria was prepping some salads.

"Don't tell Maria she's here," Katrina said.

When Katrina put the plate in front of Vivian - a filet, stuffed with chorizo, surrounded by yellow rice and a mound of steaming black beans - Santiago was sitting at her table, sipping red wine.

He had brought a half-finished bottle with him.

As Katrina pulled her hand away from the plate, Santiago grabbed her wrist and held on.

"Did you know my *gringa* is a poet?" he said to Vivian, sounding a little drunk.

"Can she recite a love poem for us?" Vivian asked him, still not looking at Katrina.

"I'm sure. *Gringa*, give us a love poem!"

Katrina tried to ease her arm away, but Santiago held fast.

"All my poems are sad," she said. "Especially the love poems. Can I have my arm back, please?"

Santiago let her go with a laugh.

"Maybe later," he said to Vivian.

Katrina turned and took a few steps before she noticed Maria standing at the back of the restaurant.

She was outside the kitchen doorway, calm and tearless, her arms at her sides. In one fist, she clutched the meat cleaver, from the other dangled a sagging slab of meat.

There were just six people left in the restaurant. Only a few of them noticed the stocky woman in the stained apron walking slowly past them, her face without makeup, her hair stuffed into a black net.

Santiago and Vivian, quietly giggling to each other, their heads close, were oblivious.

I should stop her, Katrina thought, but her feet refused to move.

Carmen, who was setting dirty dishes in the plastic hamper at the back of the restaurant, made a move to intercept Maria. But the cook glared in her direction and shook her head.

Carmen stepped back.

As Maria moved closer, Katrina could see she was holding a shiny purple hunk of calves' liver. She slammed it down onto Vivian's table, where it landed with a wet SPLAT!

Santiago and Vivian jumped back, their chairs scuffing loudly on the floor.

Maria slowly raised the cleaver high over her head.

"Please, no," Vivian pleaded.

"Maria, *por favor!*" Santiago hissed.

Maria's arm came down, the cleaver splitting the meat down the center with a sharp CRACK and throwing off flecks of blood and bits of flesh.

The blade sank deep into the wood.

Her voice was cold, her eyes focused on Santiago.

"I divorce you," Maria said.

Then she turned to Vivian.

"He is yours now," she said through clenched teeth. "*Buena suerte.*"

Maria turned back toward the kitchen, wiping her bloody hands on her apron.

Shocked diners, some with forks held aloft in mid-bite, watched Maria stride away. When she disappeared into the kitchen, their eyes swiveled back to Santiago and Vivian.

The cleaver remained stuck in the table, the handle tilted, like the hand of a clock pointed toward two. Blood and goo had splattered across Vivian's dress and the tops of her breasts.

Santiago picked up a napkin to wipe her off but Vivian screamed "NO!" and ran from the restaurant.

Santiago remained in his seat, ignoring the bloody carnage on his pale blue guayabera. With a shaky hand, he lifted the wine glass to his lips.

Maria, still in her apron, crossed the restaurant and walked out the tall, wooden door, with Carmen scurrying close behind clutching two umbellas.

"Fuck you twice!" Carmen yelled at Santiago from the door, her right arm outstretched in his direction, her middle finger pointing up.

Katrina went to the tall wooden cabinet along the back wall and took a wine glass. She walked to Santiago's table and filled her glass from his bottle. He looked at her blankly, then held up his glass. Katrina filled it to the top, finishing off the bottle.

She sat at a table by the tall windows, sipping wine and looking out at the dark Ybor streetscape. The monsoons continued, the sky in full, end-of-the-world tumult, the low rumble of the thunder giving way every few seconds to a blast of lightning that whited-out the street. It reminded Katrina of the flashes from a newspaper photographer's camera in an old black and white movie.

Words clicked by before she settled on one that she hoped wasn't too much for this moment.

"Apocalypse": *an event involving destruction or damage on an awesome or catastrophic scale.*

Katrina took another sip of wine.

She wasn't sure what was next in her young life. She did know one thing: at some point that night she would sit down at her writing desk and light two tapered white candles with a wooden match. From the top drawer, she'd gather her silver fountain pen and three sheets of heavy bond paper.

Then she would start to work on what was certain to be a very sad poem about love.

GROUND ZERO

I killed the Street Poet of Ybor.

I mean, I didn't pull a trigger or anything.

But it doesn't really matter how you kill someone. Or if what you did doesn't legally qualify as murder.

If a person dies and you're responsible, then you're a killer.

To make it worse, my crime carried no consequences.

Saint Lewis was dead, his ashes traveling by Greyhound back to his family in Missouri and I was wide awake in a Pepto-pink bathroom, praying for a sunrise still hours away.

Maybe I've spent too many months on the police beat, but I should have been handcuffed to a metal desk in a snot-green room, my skin ice blue under the fluorescents while a dog-faced detective, cuticles of sweat circling his armpits, pushed a pad and pen in my direction.

"Write down what you told me," he'd bark. "Everything. From the beginning. And then sign it. You want coffee?"

***

I met Saint Lewis before I moved to Tampa.

The Tampa Tribune had flown me in for a round of interviews, the last hurdle before a newspaper offers you a job.

In August of 1986 I was two months out of the University of New Orleans, and I'd expected to be writing for the Times-Picayune. I was a journalism major and had been editor of the college paper, but I never got even a rejection letter from my hometown newspaper.

So here I was eating a Cuban sandwich – Tampa's version of a Po Boy - in a narrow dining room papered in red brocade and lit with tiny pink lights. Paul Hogan, the Tribune's managing editor, had brought me to Ybor City's historic Columbia Restaurant for a final interview over lunch.

I ordered iced tea, but Hogan overruled me.

"He'll have a Dewer's and water. Me too," he told the tuxedoed waiter.

"You do drink, don't you?" Hogan asked. "I mean, you are from New Orleans."

"I've been known to take a sip. Occasionally," I replied, hoping I sounded clever and adult.

The blue-suited man across the table reminded me of Jack Nicholson. He was dark-haired and almost handsome, with a mouth that slipped easily into a devilish grin. I had relatives in south Georgia, so I recognized his smoky, slow-moving drawl.

The waiter returned and Hogan raised his drink in a toast.

"Here's to occasional drinking."

Hogan laughed as we tapped our glasses. Maybe I would actually get this job.

After lunch we stood on the wide sidewalk as cars eased along Seventh Avenue, the scotch putting the whole scene in slow motion. I watched Hogan light a Marlboro 100 with a silver Zippo. Semis, headed for the interstate from the Port of Tampa surged at the stoplight, like mechanical racehorses skittish in the starting gate.

Just then the poet appeared, circling us like some oddball electron.

"So, Mr. Newspaper, looks like you could use some poetry this fine day!"

The poet was a small man with a bit of a belly and eyes that refused to hold still.

"Let me give you something to cleanse your mental pores. Something to take away those nasty wrinkles around your heart. Something to make you feel as young as the day you were born."

Hogan laughed and pulled out his wallet. The poet's smile widened.

"Saint Lewis, this is Daniel Hebert from that famous party town,

New Orleans, Louisiana," Hogan said, pronouncing my name the right way – A-bear.

"Nice suit," the poet told me, his eyes darting around my brand new chocolate brown three-piece, accessorized with a wide paisley tie and spit-polished Florscheims. "Did your mama pick that out?"

Hogan looked at me and smirked. Saint Lewis was right. Dorothy Hebert had insisted her eldest son go to Tampa with "a proper job interview suit and a proper job interview haircut."

She also told me you should never lie during a job interview. I nervously pushed my hand through the shortest haircut I'd had in five years.

"I'll take the fifth-amendment on the grounds that it might be true," I told the poet.

"Well I'll drink to your mama's good taste," Saint Lewis said. "As soon as I can acquire the appropriate funding, that is. The day is young."

He kept circling, his eye now on Hogan's wallet. I noticed squiggles of an Afro emerging from the edges of a black beret and a smile so wide his mouth seemed to hold more teeth than a human was allowed. His blue button-down, tucked into baggy khakis, was threadbare and pocked with cigarette burns.

Hogan waved a five and Saint Lewis made a sad face and tilted his head left. Hogan pulled out another five and the poet's happy face returned. Saint Lewis paused so his patron could slip the bills into his breast pocket. Hogan tapped two cigarettes from his pack and stuck them behind the folded bills.

"You see those ladies over there?" Hogan said, pointing at a clutch of well-dressed women of a certain age waiting for the valet to return with their car.

"I think you should give my poem to them."

137

Saint Lewis bowed from the waist.

"Ladies!" he shouted, as he stepped toward them. "It's your lucky day!"

The woman clutched their handbags and five coiffed heads swiveled in a desperate search for the valet.

"Ladies, I'm here to give you a poem. A bouquet of nouns and verbs with a few late-blooming adjectives thrown in for color. None have ever heard it. No one else can own it. I give it to you and to you alone."

Hogan elbowed me as we watched a skinny woman, her apricot hair stiff as cotton candy, trying to wrest control of the situation from this disheveled black man. She kept turning around – never quite able to keep up with the poet.

"No! We don't have any spare change," she said sternly. "Sorry."

"Ladies, this one is pre-paid," he beamed. "It's totally free!"

Saint Lewis stopped and extended his arms. He cleared his throat with much gravely ceremony. He stared directly at the skinny ringleader, his eyes doing a herky-jerky dance.

Me – I'm a Mars Bar
and you
you're a Klondike
- cold as Pluto when I approach.
We're different planets in the
universal convenience store

Cigarettes had added a layer of sandpaper to the poet's regal baritone but his voice had the power to reach the upper balcony of a Broadway theater.

I wait on the candy counter

stiff, wrapped, ready.
Chocolate skin over
a pea-nutty center.

And there you are
Tucked in the deep
freeze your
sugary places
sealed in silver.

Can you feel it
when your hard shell
puckers?

That's me.
Calling.

Saint Lewis paused to take a big breath. The cluster of women tightened. Heads spun. WHERE IS OUR CAR?

The poet started circling again, his volume up a notch. Diners emerging onto the sidewalk stopped to stare. Saint Lewis acknowledged his audience with a nod and continued:

A few feet of linoleum can't
keep us apart.
Our passion erupts!
A ten on the
Richter scale of love that
rocks the mini-mart
of the heart.

Crash goes the candy counter.
Smash goes the deep freeze. And we
slide together
across a freshly mopped floor
until my hard
NUTTY!
bar, pierces your soft,

vanilla veil
And we lie together…

He delivered his next line like the dying witch in the Wizard of Oz:

MMMMEEEEELLLLLTING……

Until all that's left
Of us
Is a thimble-full of
sweet, white
cream…

Saint Lewis bowed deeply. As if on cue, the valet arrived behind the wheel of a golden land yacht and the women scurried to get inside.

Hogan stuffed his cigarette into his mouth and applauded. I joined him.

"Somebody needs to do a story on that guy," Hogan said. "You want to write it?"

"Is that a job offer?"

"Why the hell not?" Hogan shrugged amiably.

***

Rookie reporters at the Tribune always started on the night police beat - at least the men. New female reporters got a pass on the 6:30 p.m. to 2:30 a.m. shift because the editors — at this point all male - worried about sending a young woman into dark alleys and shaky neighborhoods at 1 in the morning.

They were probably right.

In my six months on the beat, I'd been chased by a gang of 12-year-olds armed with pool cues, nipped on the butt by a snarling pit bull, and witnessed a shoot-out in a 24-hour-diner.

The late-night hours were not great for my love life either. Since moving to Tampa in September, I'd had sex with just one woman, a 23-year-old copy editor named Grace Manson who also worked the late shift.

Grace was a lanky, sour-faced girl in black-framed bifocals, who cinched her limp brown ponytail with rubber bands. Each day she wore gray polyester slacks and mannish white blouses, buttoned up to a collar feminized by a single band of lace.

To be fair, I was no prize either, just six-feet-two-inches of bones and skin, costumed in wrinkled khaki slacks, polyester dress shirts, skinny ties and Elvis Costello glasses. Like Ichabod Crane, my Adam's apple and my nose competed to be my most distinctive feature.

But if the police beat teaches you anything, it's that after midnight crime and sex are mostly about proximity.

Each night I would hand Grace dispatches about fatal car wrecks, murdered spouses, and businessmen caught in prostitution stings. She got them edited, headlined and into the paper.

By 2:30, as the presses roared to life, we were always hungry and over-caffeinated.

Grace was just a colleague the late September night when we decided to try the eggs and sausage at a 24-hour diner a mile from the newspaper.

Grace didn't do small talk and I was too tired to take up the slack. So we sat silently, like an old married couple. I was dusting a mug of muddy decaf with Dixie Crystals when the diner's wooden door banged open and a skeletal creature in a dirty T-shirt and unlaced gym shoes fell through it.

"THIS IS A RAPERY!"

I figured he was trying to shout "THIS IS A ROBBERY," but what came out was more of a phlegmy croak, like the sound of a man who hadn't spoken all day. Instead of moving ahead with the robbery, or the rapery, the man froze, his right arm deep in the crotch of his saggy jeans.

I had taken a police department seminar on how to be a good witness and while our robber rooted around in his pants, I ran down the check-list: maybe 35-years-old; 5-feet-6 or 7; Caucasian; with a scrub-brush of sandy hair; a stub for a nose; and oddly, no eyebrows, no lashes, no stubble.

A tiny silver revolver – barely bigger than a derringer - finally emerged from his pants and he stared down at it for several seconds, apparently making sure it was actually in his hand. When his head jerked up, he saw the stumpy old counterman pointing two pearl-handled pistols at his chest.

The robber's face clenched, leaving his lips puckered and his left eye squeezed shut. His gun arm slowly unbent until the tiny pistol was pointed at the linoleum.

I hadn't paid attention to the counterman when we came in, but now I saw his ruddy jowls and square skull were carpeted in tiny spikes of white stubble. The dark stains on his white apron could have been blood, but were likely just ketchup.

Never taking his eyes off the intruder, the counterman slowly raised the pistols to the ceiling and squeezed both triggers.

It sounded like two grenades had detonated in the narrow, tin-walled diner.

Through windows yellowed by years of bacon grease, we watched our ragged robber disappear like an Olympic sprinter across the asphalt.

"Nothing to worry about folks. They call 'em crack-heads, but they don't scare me," the old man said calmly, as the pistols went back under the counter. "Anybody need more coffee?"

We finished eating in silence, our eggs now flavored with the semi-sweet aroma of gunpowder. I noticed Grace's hand was shaking when she pulled a wallet from her purse.

I had barely sat down in Grace's tiny Honda when she was on me like wallpaper, her tongue thrusting deep into my mouth.

Moments later we were upstairs in her garage apartment, behind a Hyde Park mansion, grappling on an unmade single bed. She didn't seem to notice the telephone that jangled insistently on the bedside table.

"Should you get that?" I asked, hoping she would. Grace was a determined kisser and my tongue ached from all the thrusts and parries. I was also frustrated by a reluctant clasp on her bra.

"It's my fiancée. He'll call back."

The fingers of her right hand had been digging deep into my butt. She let go and deftly popped the clip on her bra, freeing two demitasse breasts.

"He won't come over?"

"He's in Daytona Beach so I don't think so," she said, as she pushed my head down onto a taut, peach-colored nipple circled by a single black hair.

And that was that.

Some nights we spent in her apartment. Some nights she came to my walk-up above the Ritz Theater in Ybor. We shared coffee each morning, then didn't speak again until we started our shift. On weekends, she went to Daytona or her fiancée came to Tampa to sleep in the bed I had occupied the night before.

Neither of us had any complaints about the routine. Grace was planning a June wedding and I was focused on proving to Paul Hogan that he hadn't made a mistake hiring me.

To do that I needed stories nobody else had. And I quickly figured out the best ally a reporter can have is a friendly, talkative shift commander – the captains or lieutenants who ride the desk through the long nights. They heard all the stories and got a first look at all the reports.

Five nights a week, if I wasn't out at a crime scene, I loitered in shabby offices not much wider than a hallway. A shift commander – always a man - sat in a cushioned chair that squeaked when he leaned back. The guest chair, where I sat, was hollow metal and crammed so close my knees touched the desk.

Terry Childers, my favorite commander, was a Tennessee transplant. He shared Paul Hogan's relaxed southern cadence but he was fair and freckled, with a shaving brush moustache, and the swagger of an elite athlete. He loved telling stories about the young lawbreakers he chased down on foot back before he was promoted to desk duty.

"What's your price?" I asked him one night when the radio that occasionally crackled on his desk carried no urgent calls. "How much to cross the line?"

It was a game I played with shift commanders to kill the long night hours. What would it take for them to go rogue?

Chiders seemed to have already thought of it.

"It's 3 a.m. and I'm cruising behind an armored car that just picked up the cash from the dog track. Usually about 250 K in small bills. Untraceable. The truck hits a bump, the back door opens and a duffle bag of money comes flying out."

Childers sipped his coffee.

"Now it's in my trunk and nobody knows about it but me. So…. maybe I'd turn it in and maybe I wouldn't. I certainly don't plan to tell a reporter what I'd do in that situation."

I had a mailbox at the station, where the police information officer left crime alerts and press releases. Some nights when I started my shift I'd find a photo-copy of a police report with the word - "*Hmmmmm?*" – scrawled across the top.

The reports were my gifts from Childers.

One *"Hmmmm?"* led me to a former crack-head who decided to take some swings with a metal post at the bike-riding drug dealers in his neighborhood. They responded by putting a 22 slug in the soft flesh of his butt.

Another described chaos at a high school cheerleading tryout. The father of a girl who didn't make the squad had fired a shot at the father of the head cheerleader.

In both cases, the wounds were minor, but the stories were colorful and nobody had them but me.

I started seeing my byline on the front of the metro section.

The days those features appeared, Hogan would appear at my desk with a cup of coffee from the office vending machine.

"Pretty good tale" is what he always said, setting the coffee down on any clear spot he could find on my paper-strewn desk.

The coffee was terrible; the praise was delicious.

"I'd like to write about that Ybor poet now, if that's okay with you," I told Hogan one evening after he set the coffee on my desk.

"You do that. Just make sure to stick with his cleaner material," Hogan said. "Remember, we're a family newspaper."

***

"Come in. Come in. I've been waiting for you all morning," Saint Lewis hollered from the back of the house, his baritone carrying through the screen door and onto the front porch. "In fact, I started the celebration without you."

The poet lived in a casita in a squalid neighborhood just east of the historic district. Most of the old immigrant shacks on his street were boarded up or should have been.

But the poet's house was a wildflower blooming among the weeds.

The porch was solid, with two Adirondack chairs and an orange crate for a table. I pulled open the screen door.

"Back here," he called, from the far end of a center hallway that led from front to back.

His shotgun shack was clean; the furniture old but functional. Vivid pastel renderings of Van Gogh-like flowers – all signed in a swirling cursive *Saint Lewis*!
– were thumb-tacked to the walls.

It wasn't the home I expected for a wild-eyed guy who made his money selling poetry on the street.

His kitchen spanned the back of the old house. The morning sun, pouring in from six tall windows, painted the walls, cabinets and the floor with geometric boxes of light set inside shadows.

One box of light fell across a wooden table where Saint Lewis sat before two highball glasses and a half-empty pint bottle. He smiled when I approached, but was apparently too far into the bottle to stand up.

"Let me fix you a drink," he said, as he hoisted the pint. "Bean's Eight Star Kentucky Whiskey. It's not what you'd call top-shelf liquor, but it satisfies nonetheless."

"Later," I told him; it was just after 11 a.m.

"I thought maybe so. There's coffee on the stove."

146

A silver espresso maker sat on a burner, next to a ceramic mug with *YBOR* etched into the handle. As I reached for it, a tiny red-haired dog - mostly bones covered by a thin carpet of bristle – shot from under the table and began to furiously hump my ankle.

"That's Easy," the poet said. "Just kick him off you. He won't mind. He's a horny little bastard."

"Has he been fixed?" I asked "That tends to slow 'em down."

"Fixed? Please! How would you like it if your parents snipped your little wienie? It's barbaric. Be what God made you. That's my philosophy."

"Can't argue there. You got sugar?"

"If God wanted coffee sweet, he'd have made it that way," he said forcefully, then he shook his head. "Sorry, I tend to preach sometimes. I believe you'll find Yogi in the cupboard."

Pulling open a cabinet, I found dishes neatly stacked and glasses upside down on yellow shelf paper. Behind another door was a bag of Uncle Ben's rice, a jar of peanut butter, a box of Cheerios and a plastic bear filled with honey.

"I live in Ybor too and I gotta say, your place is much nicer than mine," I told him, as a golden straw of sweetness arced from Yogi's head into my mug.

I told people I was drawn to Ybor by the scene – the artists, the parties, the boho vibe – but I made a little over $250 a week and Ybor, with its termites, bad plumbing and roaches the size of rodents, was what I could afford.

Saint Lewis laughed, showing off that mouthful of teeth.

"You didn't realize there was so much money in the poetry business, right?"

"I can't lie," he continued. "Angels look after me. I likely don't deserve it, but I do accept it."

From my backpack, I took out a tape recorder and set it on the table. Then I retrieved a pack of Marlboro 100s that I'd purchased on the way over.

"You mind if I tape our visit?" I asked as I pushed the cigarettes toward him.

Saint Lewis spun the red plastic ribbon off, then tapped the bottom of the pack on the table.

"No secrets here. My book is completely open."

Over the next hour I learned a lot.

Saint Lewis was the pen name of Thaddeus Washington Lewis, the youngest child of a large middle-class family from St. Louis. His father was a high school English teacher. His mother a guidance counselor.

"The Saint part was my nickname in our family. That's how I learned about irony. – which I believe is the one essential ingredient of good poetry. As a kid, I was anything but saintly."

"I'd love to hear more about that."

My request sent Saint Lewis into a story I was sure he had told more than once.

"Can a black family have a black sheep? If so, then you're looking at him. We were seven children and the truth is momma should have stopped at six. I arrived with a long list of … conditions," he said, making quote marks with his fingers around 'conditions'. "And now my family and I are, I guess the word is, es-stranged. That's 'cause my siblings are es-tablished and I'm just strange!"

He laughed at his own joke, then continued:

"My sister, Thelma – a good Christian woman - makes sure wherever I'm living, the rent and the light bill get paid. I think of it as my inheritance."

"Does she pay for a housekeeper too? You're place is so..."

"Clean? That's my doing. Mother taught me that cleanliness is next to godliness. God left the building a long time ago, but a man needs to believe in something. I believe in cleanliness … and poetry."

I heard about short stays at three colleges and a county jail in Delaware, and a bus trip to Miami to track down an old girlfriend.

"Due to an unfortunate misunderstanding, I was asked to exit the bus when we stopped in Tampa. So here I am."

Saint Lewis stood with his hand flat on the table, taking a few seconds to gain his balance, then went for some fresh ice from the freezer. He opened a kitchen drawer and pulled out a manila folder stuffed with yellow, legal sized paper. He dropped it in front of me with a loud plop.

He said it was a novel about his time in jail – "It's a lot Dostoyevsky and a little Malcolm X." I scanned the first few pages. They were dense with scribbled words. Each paragraph made sense, but there seemed to be nothing that linked one paragraph to the next.

"So you see," he said, as he slowly settled himself back in his chair, "I'm a professional writer who keeps himself afloat with my street corner verses. I'm no beggar. People give me something green and I give them something golden in return."

I checked my recorder to make sure the tape was still turning.

"So how do you know who wants a poem and who doesn't?" I asked.

Saint Lewis reached across the small table, his hand patting mine

149

gently, his skin rough but comforting, like the feel of washed-out blue jeans.

"People don't know they want a poem until you give it to them. But some are more amenable than others. In general terms, women are more amenable than men. Blacks more amenable than whites. My ideal customer is a pretty young black woman who has just stepped out of a small red car. As soon as I see one of those, I know I'm about to start versifying."

***

My story about the poet ran on 1-A of the Sunday paper – my best play ever, and featured a haunting portrait of the poet's weathered face – his eyes half-lidded, as smoke swirled up from the end of a Marlboro. The story jumped inside, illustrated with a shot of Saint Lewis in the parking lot of the Blue Ribbon grocery sharing a poem with a giggling young black woman, while her three pre-school age children danced and clapped.

Hogan shook my hand Monday afternoon when I showed up for work. My interoffice message queue brimmed with compliments from other writers and editors.

I loved the praise but I knew I hadn't told the whole story.

The Saint Lewis I described was a lively eccentric. An entertainer. A curiosity for sure - but safe around pets and children.

What I'd left out was what happened to him as the day gave way to dusk and one drink became four. When he changed from the happy poet to the belligerent drunk.

I left out the chilly night at an east Ybor flophouse that smelled of urine and worse, when he stood in a circle of thin, jumpy men as an aluminum foil pipe was passed around, each puff lit by a match from below. Childers had told me about a new type of cheap cocaine – in crystal form – called *Crack*, but I'd never seen it up close until that night.

When we walked out onto the street later, the poet's eyes twittered like a pair of hummingbirds and his ideas raced to catch them and EVERYTHING HAD TO BE DONE RIGHT NOW!

Fragments of verse shot from his mouth like the harsh staccato of bullets from a machine gun. Standing on Seventh Avenue in a block of abandoned buildings, I encouraged him to go home and write this stuff down. I aimed him in that direction. He strode away like Shakespeare on speed, his black trench coat flaring in the wind, his swinging arms and clawing fingers adding emphasis to a torrent of words I could still hear a block away.

Monday night I told Grace the whole story and she listened quietly, her head on an adjoining pillow.

"It's a feature story in a daily newspaper," she said, when I finally stopped talking. "A snapshot with the ugly parts airbrushed out. That's what we do."

***

Tuesday morning I stopped by Saint Lewis' house with four copies of Sunday's front page.

The man who stepped onto the porch to greet me was the happy poet. He wrapped me in a bear hug, then offered coffee.

"Everybody wanted a poem Sunday. I made $160 and one lady even had me autograph her copy of the paper! Apparently now I'm not only a published poet, but a celebrated one."

"Just doing my job," I told him.

"Hey, I was invited by some young writers to the open mic at that bookstore – Free Birds? Three Birds? If you're there this evening by 9, you'll catch the good stuff."

I shook my head.

"Gotta work the mean streets," I said.

"Tomorrow morning then? We'll have coffee and I'll tell you about my adventures when I was crewing a riverboat out of Saint Louis. Huck had nothing on me, I assure you."

"Maybe later this week," I told him. "I've got a lot of interviews set up in the next few days. But I'll be back soon for coffee."

But of course, I wasn't coming back. I had done my story and was moving on to the next one. Three days and nights in Saint Lewis' world had been enough for me.

But the poet wasn't ready to let me go.

He had my telephone number and after a week went by and I didn't visit, he began calling five or six times a day, always suggesting more plans, more stories I could write about him as I politely dodged and weaved.

The morning he woke me up with a 7 a.m. call, I snapped.

"Listen, I'm sorry. But it was a story for the newspaper. It was business. I've moved on to the next story. You need to move on too."

I heard the phone click off; the drone of the dial tone rang in my ear like a rebuke. Later that morning, as I made coffee, I noticed a figure lingering in the alley below my kitchen window.

Saint Lewis was staring up at me. Not knowing what else to do, I waved. He didn't wave back. Instead, he shook his head and walked slowly down the alley.

***

Living one flight up from Seventh Avenue, it was easy to get pulled into the Ybor scene.

152

My neighbor Cilla, an art history major and part-time waitress, introduced me to the crew of artists around the bar at Rough Riders. When my Trib editor rejected a story on an El Goya drag queen, I got it published in Ybor's monthly art paper, *Tabloid*, under my NOLA pen name Royal Street. That story led me to David Audet, who designed *Tabloid* and also ran *Ground Zero*, a performance space a few blocks north of Seventh, where some USF theater grads, working as *School of Night,* delivered profane, gender-bending sketch comedy.

David wanted to produce a night of storytelling at *Ground Zero*.

"Maybe you could do talk about one of your street characters," he suggested. "What do you think?"

I didn't think of myself as an actor, but I'd played one of Stanley's card buddies in a college production of "Streetcar" and taken a few theater classes. Both moves were less about art and more about meeting girls in the drama department. But I figured I could do this.

I went back to my tape recordings of Saint Lewis and two weeks later, I handed over a 15-minute story about my time with Saint Lewis. It had some elements of my newspaper piece, but I was free to go darker and deeper, not just about Saint Lewis, but about my guilt at loving and leaving him.

David liked it. Soon I was part of a three-night run of stories, performances and poems at *Ground Zero*, sharing the bill with a drag queen named Maria von Tramp, whose one-woman show was called *The Sound of Muzak,* and Barry Gary, who wrote epic-length poems that chronicled the erotic and political adventures of an oversexed couple named Ron and Nancy.

I decided to invite Saint Lewis. I knew he'd enjoy hearing a story about himself. I also thought it would be an easy way to apologize for treating him badly six months earlier.

I was wary as I approached his house on a steaming morning in June, but when Saint Lewis pushed open the screen door, it was as if nothing negative had ever passed between us.

"Paper boy! What a treat for my eyes. Come on in. I might have some coffee inside."

He was unshaven and thinner than I remembered and his house was a mess: clothes tossed on the couch, rags and newspapers on the floor, dirty dishes stacked in the sink. In an ash try on the kitchen table I saw a hand-wrapped foil pipe and a half-empty pack of matches.

"How's the book coming?" I asked, as the poet did a jittery search of his empty cupboards for a bag of coffee he never found.

"It's percolating. All up here," he said, a hooked finger pecking at his head. "Just need to get it down on paper. It's good. My best stuff. I know I've got some coffee here somewhere."

"I've had plenty. Don't worry about me. I just wanted to invite you to a show tonight at *Ground Zero*. You know the place?"

Saint Lewis' head swiveled in my direction and I saw a switch had been flipped. His body turned in a series of short jerks, his eyes searching the room for some hidden intruder.

"Don't like the name. Don't like the place. There once, just passing by. It smelled like Nagasaki in the morning."

He snuggled his arms across his chest like a man chilled by an icy gust.

"It's really not a bad place," I said, not sure where the name had taken him.

"It's ground zero," he said, coming closer and bending his head toward mine. "Smells like death is calling you from down the alley."

***

My Ground Zero show was scheduled for nine. When I reached for the door at seven, I stopped outside and sniffed. I caught a whiff of roasted coffee and a hint of stale beer, pretty much what you smelled anywhere in Ybor, but nothing else.

I pulled open the steel door and heard Saint Lewis inside, shouting in his belligerent, late-night staccato.

"You got no power over me, white man," he bellowed. "No damn power at all."

I had managed to keep the criminals and misfits I wrote about separate from the friends I was making in Ybor, but now my two worlds were colliding.

David – an artist with the body of a Port Tampa stevedore - had grabbed a fistful of Saint Lewis' blue dress shirt and held him at arm's length. David turned in my direction, his voice surprisingly calm.

"Either you get him out of here or I'm throwing him out," he said.

"Tell this cracker asshole who I am!" Saint Lewis' voice rose even louder when he saw me, his eyes in the full crazy dance. "I'm the Street Poet of Ybor dammit! This show is all about me! All about me! Tell him!"

I was able to pull Saint Lewis out the front door to the sidewalk, but he continued to rant. Finally, I grabbed his chin and swiveled his face into mine.

"LOOK AT ME!" I shouted like a drill sergeant. "This isn't going to work. I'll bring you back another night. But now, we've got to get you out of here. OK?"

Saint Lewis swallowed hard and took a long, crusty breath, then hacked up something into his hand. He rubbed his hand absently on the front of his shirt and shook his head. He was still jittering but I felt him slowing down, like a spinning top just starting to wobble.

"Let's get you home now," I said calmly. "Some beer, maybe? Some cigarettes? You'll feel better and we'll talk tomorrow about all this. OK?"

Saint Lewis nodded but then he crumpled like a rag doll in my arms, his eyes rolling back in his head.

I held the dead weight of him and looked desperately for help, but we were alone on the sidewalk. Now I smelled it – a rancid gumbo of blood and beer and something like rotting eggs – but the smell was coming off the poet, not the place. I felt a gag forming in the back of my throat as my knees bent under this weight.

Then, just like that, his head came up and the poet rose like Lazarus stepping stiffly from the grave.

"Thirsty," he muttered.

"We'll get you something on the way home."

With my arm wrapped around his waist, Saint Lewis and I hobbled down Seventh Avenue toward his house. I heard him repeating some mad mantra in a garbled whisper. Slowly, his voice grew stronger.

"Ground zero. Sprouted that big mushroom of shit. Scorched the earth. Ground zero. Nagasaki in the morning. Can you smell it?"

We were walking past the Ritz Theater, and a block of empty storefronts.
He stopped and pushed away from me.

"This, this, this…it's all ground zero," he said, waving his arms around.

"All ground zero. Total destruction. Nothing left but the smell. Nothing left but the smell."

The poet's face clenched. Painted by the neon of the Ritz marquee, violet tears glistened against a slate gray cheek. Inside the chest of

156

this 50-year-old showman was the pounding heart of a frightened child.

"Please Mr. Paper Boy, please don't leave me at ground zero. Okay?"

"I won't."

"Promise me, paper boy. Promise me."

"I promise. It'll be okay. Let's get you home."

There was a bodega a few blocks from his house. As I settled him on a bench outside, he clutched at my arm.

"Don't leave me here..."

"I'm just going in the store to get you some beer. Some smokes. Okay? I'm coming right back."

I unbent his fingers that had tightened around my wrist.

Inside, I bought a six-pack of Old Milwaukee and a pack of Marlboro 100s. The store had no dog food, but it did have a few cans of beef stew. I bought one for the poet and one for Easy, the red dog.

Outside, dusk had settled over Ybor, the jagged streets and the flat sky were buffed in charcoal.

"Thaddeus, it's time to go home,' I said, thinking there might be some comfort in hearing his boyhood name. "How about it? Let's take you home."

He nodded. I helped him stand.

***

After I settled him on his sofa, I put the cigarettes and one of the beers on the coffee table. In the kitchen, I rinsed off a bowl from the kitchen sink and dumped in the stew. When I set it on the floor, Easy came scampering; his fuzzy face disappeared deep inside the dish.

I opened the refrigerator to stash the beer, but suddenly I was back on that sidewalk reeling from the smell of rot. I slammed it shut, and stumbled to an open window, exhaling the stench and taking in the thick June air.

When I knew I wasn't going to vomit, I headed back down the hallway. I had to get out of this house. Thankfully, when I reached the living room, Saint Lewis had regained some strength.

"Home of the brave," he said, looking up at me. "Maybe a little drink and a smoke. That'll be good."

"There's some food on the kitchen counter. You should eat," I said, my hand on the doorknob. "I'll come check on you tomorrow. I've got to get back to the theater now."

He reached up weakly and waved for me to come shake his hand. When we shook, his grip tightened and he pulled me close. I tried not to breathe him in.

"Remember your promise."

I wasn't sure exactly what Saint Lewis wanted from me, but I was desperate to break away from his needy grasp and those sunken, jittery eyes.

"I promise."

He loosened his grip and almost smiled.

"Okay paper boy. Okay."

***

I didn't pick up the paper until I got to work Monday evening.

I had spent the day nursing the hangover I earned at the Sunday night cast party at El Goya. Never try to keep up when a drag queen decides to order tequila shots.

But I was happy enough as I sipped my first *café con leche* at 2 p.m. and thought back to the weekend.

Five rows of metal folding chairs were full each night. I stood in a single white spot, doing my best to capture the poet and his world. I got laughs in the right places and applause at the end. I never thought I had an addictive personality, but the audience and the applause grabbed me by the lapels and wouldn't let go. I loved it. I wanted more.

Grace came on Saturday night with her fiancée – a pale, balding guy named Jeff who now knew me as Grace's "friend from work."

I'd talked about Saint Lewis all weekend, but the desperate man I left on the couch Friday night had been far from my thoughts.

I made a second cup of coffee Monday afternoon and started jotting notes about other characters from my reporting. I wanted to put together a collection of monologues for David.

***

I made it to the paper by 5. My shift didn't officially start until 6:30, so I sat near the vending machines in the break room and scanned the metro sections from the weekend to see what I had missed.

The story was on the front page of Sunday's Metro section. It was a one-column news item under the headline *"Man dies in Ybor house fire."*

TAMPA - Firefighters found the body of Thaddeus Lewis inside his house after neighbors reported smelling smoke early Saturday morning. The 51-year-old Ybor City resident had apparently fallen asleep while smoking a cigarette, fire officials said.

Several empty beer cans were around his feet, leading investigators to believe the victim was intoxicated.

The weekend reporter, a college intern, hadn't looked up Thaddeus Lewis in the clips, so he didn't identify him as *The Street Poet of Ybor.*

I ran downstairs and drove like a madman to the poet's house. The fire hadn't done much damage to the exterior. Only the yellow police tape on the door indicated any change from when I'd fled on Friday night. But peering through a window, I saw the couch was charred and the walls around it were black from smoke. Up close, I inhaled the acrid stench that remains after a fire – like Nagasaki in the morning.

My apartment was the closest phone. From there, I called the shift commander.

"It was your guy, wasn't it?" Childers asked.

"Yeah, the poet," I said.

"Well, it's not a glamorous way to die, but it's not painful. You fall asleep. You don't wake up."

"There was a dog," I said. "Anything in there about the dog?"

I could hear him turning through the report.

"Animal control picked up a small dog of indeterminate breed," he said. "Been at the pound 48 hours by now so…"

"Dammit!"

I told Childers about Friday night. About leaving the poet with six beers, a pack of cigarettes.

"So basically you killed him," Childers said. "And his little dog too."

"I guess I did."

"Sounds like he was headed that way already."

"What should I do now?"

"I'd book you for murder, but we're pretty busy tonight. So I'd say – forget it. Get on with your life."

***

My life was moving forward quickly.

A new reporter had been hired fresh from the University of South Florida journalism school. He'd spend the next six months or so on the night shift. Thanks to my feature stories, I had leapt over the boring government beats that normally came next. I would be a swing-shift reporter, working noon to 9, free to follow the best stories of the day.

That Monday night, after our shifts, Grace and I ended our affair. She was off to Daytona on Friday for her wedding. I offered to take her back to the old diner with the trigger-happy counterman, but she shook her head and we ate our last late-night meal at a well-lit Denny's.

We made love afterwards in her single bed, both of us frantic and hungry and pushing to get to some place that seemed just out of reach, while her white wedding dress – sheathed in clear plastic - hung from a hook on the closet door.

I woke before dawn and listened to Grace snoring gently. Her window unit was throbbing, but I was soaked in sweat. In her pink-tiled bathroom, I splashed cold water on my face, then gazed at my dripping mug in the medicine cabinet mirror.

I was searching for some crease, some scar or scab. But staring back at me was a familiar 24-year-old face with sleep-caked eyes, a crooked knuckle of a nose and spikes of hair jutting like palmettos.

I had pushed the poet out of my head while I worked, but as I stared into Grace's mirror he came back in dreamlike detail: the slaughterhouse smell as he collapsed against me; the metronome twitch of his eyes as he begged for my promise; the icy stalks of his fingers encircling my hand as I pulled away.

You think you can step into someone's world and then step right out when you want to. It's not as easy as that.

I slipped back into the tiny bed, and Grace rolled in my direction, folding a warm leg over mine. I pulled her close and her head settled on my shoulder. As I felt her breath pulse on my neck, a new thought began to form.

If I put all of this together just right I'd have one hell of a story.

LION MAN

I should tell you, if you are going to write about me, my real name is
Morris Simmons, but everybody calls me The Lion Man.

See, my name is Morris, like the cat. And I'm a Leo, like the lion.

Lion. Cat. It all just figures in.

I wear lion clothes. I got lion jewelry. I got a lion mane.

I'm the Lion Man!

I play guitar with CLAW. At least I used to, but that's another story that I'm still too pissed off to discuss.

Anyway, you wanna know about that night?

Okay. I admit I was pissed off. I had a big blowup with Gina – that's my EX-girlfriend.

She said she was "tired of me accusing her of everything. Why didn't I trust her?"

All I ask is why she's always going off to work early and coming home late? It's not like Scarlet's strip club is such a fuckin' resort you can't wait to get there and start dancin'.

Am I right?

So she yells and I yell and maybe take a swing, but I was just trying to get her attention.

I've never hit her.

And that chick has beaten the shit out of me on numerous occasions. One night, I took a steak knife outta her hand just before she stuck me with it.

Fuckin' Cuban chicks man. They're like time bombs with tits. This is my last fuckin' Cuban chick and my last stripper.

Strippers are nuts too.

So she kicks me out and I walk home – we live maybe three blocks apart – but I get back to my shotgun shack and I got no keys.

I march back up the old brick street to her place, but she's gone. Lights out. Locks on. Nothing but her fat, white cat staring back at me through the window, smiling, like he's in and I'm out.

So I come back here and crawl through that window, scraping the shit out of my knee. And now I'm really pissed.

I drink one, maybe two Colt 45s. I drink 'em quick, which I know is a mistake, but my knee hurts like hell.

That's when I hear the bicycle dudes. I mean, more of less, this neighborhood is crack all night long. Dudes on bicycles going up and down. Cars stopping. Like some kinda druggie drive-thru.

That's north Ybor man, all of it.

In the not too distant future I'm getting out of here. Moving out to the 'burbs – somewhere like Tampa Palms. Building a lot of new houses in Tampa Palms.

See, when I'm not playing music, I do carpeting. Custom installation.

Look at this carpet in here. I mean, it looks like shit now because Gina's cats used it for a litter box. But feel it. Under your feet, I mean.

 Soft, right? It's the pad.

That's the fuckin' secret of carpeting.

Anyways, back to the bicycle dudes. I know 'em all. Used to be their best customer. I'm not proud of it. For about nine months you coulda called my band Morris and the Fuckin' Crackheads.

I blame Florida, man.

And my ex-wife.

She talked me into moving down her in '82 with the baby. Said we'd be close to her folks. But you can't make any money down here. You just get drunk and fucked up and …

Don't get me started talking about my marriage.

So like I say, I quit crack, but these bicycle dudes keep coming down the street.

My street!

They're like the fuckin' ice cream man or the goddamn Avon Lady.

So that night, I just said:

"That's it. It's time the Lion Man shows 'em who's the boss of this fuckin' street."

Remember *Walking Tall?*

Buford Pusser and his baseball bat? That just popped into my head that night.

It was time for The Lion Man to walk tall.

I go outside and yank a metal fence post out of the ground and I'm in the middle of the street, swinging like I'm George Brett in the on-deck circle.

I'm yelling:

"ROADBLOCK! DETOUR! COME ON, BRING ME A BICYCLE DUDE! BATTER UP, BABY! BATTER UP!"

I mean, it's two in the morning and porch lights are going on all over the neighborhood. Everybody's like:

"What the fuck's up?"

There's no moon and the streetlight is flickering on and off.

It flicks on and I see a bicycle dude peddle up. He stops at the corner. Then it goes out.

When it flicks on, he's a little closer.

It flicks again and he's even closer. And I think I see him smiling.

So I'm yelling even louder:

"COME ON! COME ON! IT'S MY STREET NOW, BABY! THE LION MAN IS GONNA EAT YOUR ASS ALIVE!"

It was right about that point when he shot me.

I didn't hear it. Just felt something like a hot wire on my back.

Suddenly, I'm on the pavement and I'm fading in and out.

I remember crawling up to a door and I'm yelling:

"HE SHOT ME!"

I remember cops and ambulances and lights spinning.

I open my eyes one time and I'm staring up at the trees and the leaves are all on fire. Hundreds of leaves, all flaming red, like I've passed out in hell's front yard.

I close my eyes real tight and there's my mom leaning over me wearing this fur jacket – you know, with the squinty fox face and those tiny black eyes staring down at me – and I say:

"Mom, I'm dying!"

And she says:

"Morris, don't die right now. Your father and I are late for dinner at the officer's club. You wait until we get back."

And I say:

"But mom, I'm dying right now!"

I wasn't, of course.

Just one shot with a .22.

Slug's still stuck to my rib.

I come home from the hospital and my place is all smashed up. They cut up my speakers. Crushed my Stratocaster.

Could'a been the bicycle dudes. Or this other guy who was mad at me for messing with his girlfriend.

Worst thing is, whoever did it, they smashed my trophies. All of 'em.

Look at this. You remember the *Ford Punt, Pass and Kick* contest? You remember that?

My mother lied about my age and got me in.

So it's 1967 and I'm 12 - well, 13 - standing on the 50-yard-line at Lambeau Field, and I won first place. *Punt, Pass and Kick*, man! Every kid wanted to win that and I won.

So that's what you wanted to know?

I did it. Probably wouldn't do it again.

All I got to show for my trouble is a bill from Tampa General for 4,271 dollars and 87 cents.

But hey, at least now everybody in this part of Ybor knows what it sounds like WHEN THE LION MAN ROARS!

I wrote a song about it. You wanna hear it?

I'd play it for you but my guitar is smashed.

Anyway, it's like a Metallica song. You know, that hard beat coming down like a jack hammer:

"BULLET IN THE BACK - GET ON THE RIGHT TRACK.

 BULLET IN THE BACK - GET ON THE RIGHT TRACK.

BULLET IN THE BACK, UHH!

BULLET IN THE BACK, OW!"

So whadda ya think?

ALMOST HAPPY

Angel's first word that frigid February morning was "FUCK!" What else do you say when wake up for the third time in a week with your sheets soaked in sweat?

Settling into the dampness, Angel tried to recall the last morning he had awakened without a lump of dread churning like a bad meal in the pit of his stomach.

Noche Buena at his mom's bungalow in West Tampa? Angel remembered being almost happy then, which was about as good as he ever allowed himself to feel.

He sat up in bed, pulling his mother's knitted afghan around him and let his mind wander back two months.

His *Noche Buena* always started on Dec. 23 when he showed up around 5 p.m. to help his mother prepare for the holiday party. That night had developed its own rituals and traditions.

Carmen Torres and her only son shared Spanish bean soup and hot Cuban bread at her tiny kitchen table while she ran through a list with the names of relatives and their Christmas presents, scrawled in tiny block letters on a yellow legal pad.

"And I hope you didn't spend a lot of money on me this year," she told him. "I don't need a thing."

"Just the usual," Angel told her. "It's fun shopping for you."

Angel knew his mother liked opening his indulgent gifts, especially with all the relatives looking on. Outside in his car, wrapped in the best ribbon and holiday paper he could find, was a large linen tablecloth – specially ordered to fit her 16-seat dining room table - and two dozen linen napkins, with sterling silver rings engraved with her initials.

After dinner, they sipped Harvey's Bristol Crème from cut crystal wine glasses etched with a single snowflake; a set of twelve and a matching decanter had been last year's present.

Carmen wore a red and white snowman sweater she had knitted herself. Her frosted hair was freshly sculpted in a style that reminded Angel of the swirled fondant icing on a wedding cake. Angel always thought his mom was beautiful and that hadn't changed now that she was in her 60s. Barely five-feet tall, she could still fit into her wedding dress. The skin over her heart-shaped cheekbones was soft and unwrinkled. She wore no makeup, her only beauty treatment a nightly dousing in Oil of Olay.

After dinner, Angel played *Silent Night* and *Deck the Halls* on the family's ebony upright as his mom sang along.

"Thank you, baby. You know that's why your dad and I paid for those piano lessons, so you'd play my Christmas songs."

Angel nodded. He knew that because she told him every Christmas.

When the singing was done, they strung the lights, then hung crocheted Santas, angels and wooden toy soldiers on the spindly limbs of the tree she got for nothing by waiting until just before Christmas when the lots were shutting down.

"What are they gonna do, ship it back up north? Mulch it?" she asked that afternoon, as he lifted the spiky tree out of her trunk. "Better they give it to a little old Cuban widow for *Noche Buena*."

That night he slept in his childhood bedroom.

The single bed, the wooden desk, the dancing hula girl lamp, and the posters on the wall were unchanged in the 10 years he'd been living on his own. There was Liza in her leather bustier and bowler from *Cabaret*, Yul Brynner as the scowling King of Siam, his hairless chest framed in maroon silk and gold lame, and Sinatra and Brando shooting dice in their Kodachrome suits from *Guys and Dolls*.

"Angel, you warm enough?"

She had slipped into his room, as he knew she would, just as he turned off the light.

With the extra blankets she had spread on his bed and the waves of fuel-oil heat pouring from a metal grid in the hallway floor, he felt a little like tomorrow's pig roasting in his uncle's special oven. The temperature on this Florida night had dropped only to the low 60s.

When she was asleep, he'd toss the blankets to the floor and crack

171

the window.

"I'm fine, Mom," he said. "Merry Christmas."

"Merry Christmas, baby," she said, her fingers finding his toes under the covers and giving them a pinch and a shake, just like she had done almost every night of his boyhood.

At noon on Christmas Eve, his Uncle Peter, a bow-legged, bantam-weight Cuban cowboy who owned a dairy east of Tampa, arrived in his faded blue pickup, with Lena, his tall, well-fed wife, and, in the truck-bed, a whole suckling pig and his *Caja China*, a corrugated metal cooking box with separate compartments for the pig and the hot coals.

That night, as Angel sat in a dining room lit by Christmas candles, savoring the moist pork, with rice and black beans, sprinkled with bits of raw onion, the long wooden table packed tight with boisterous aunts and uncles and cousins, the grandkids shouting from a nearby card table, and Mario Lanza singing *Ave Maria* on his mom's crappy little record player, he was almost happy.

It was the kind of almost-happy he felt on earlier *Noche Buenas* when his dad and his *abuelos* were still alive and he was a frail, stick-figure kid with a crooked smile and spiky black hair that no brush could tame, a boy who secretly hoped the shoebox-sized present with his name on it under the glittering tree was a Barbie.

***

Even though he was expecting it, the leaden jangle of the phone startled him.

"Hi, Mom," he said.

"Angel, are you warm enough in that place? I'm worried."

As this February in 1987 was winding down, a cold front had rushed through Florida, which always meant at least one day of drizzling rain

172

and temperatures in the high 30s. The icy air seeping through the termite-eaten frames of his windows was too much for the toaster-sized box glowing red in a corner of his apartment.

"I'm warm like toast, Mom," he lied. "That heater you gave me is doing the trick."

"You know you can come home when it gets cold like this."

"I'm fine. We got the memorial for Frankie Capitano tonight in the club. I've got to get everything ready."

"That poor boy. So young. I sent a note to his mom. I put your name on it, too."

"Thanks. I better run. Lots to do. But I'll see you Sunday for Mass."

"You're staying for lunch, right? I'm making boliche and Aunt Angie will be here with her new gentleman."

"The one with the bad toupee and the limp?"

"He's a very nice man, Angel. Much better than your Uncle Junior, rest his soul. Now promise me you'll be careful. Ybor City is dangerous these days."

"I will. Don't worry. See you Sunday."

Ybor City, where his mother and father had grown up, wasn't really "dangerous these days", just deserted, a home for fringe dwellers – artists, writers, drag queens – and their haunts – a porn theater, a storefront gallery, a gay bar.

Angel's third-floor perch had once been an office for *Las Novedades*, a restaurant where immigrants and their children splurged on birthdays and anniversaries.

Now the Mediterranean revival building was home to *El Goya*, a vast nightclub with themed rooms – *Leather Lounge, Cowpunks, Gay Paree!* –

wrapping a pulsing disco. Four nights a week, crowds packed into a back bar, outfitted with a stage and a fashion-show runway for full-scale drag reviews.

Angel's official job title was choreographer, but he called himself the "Chief Bitch Wrangler."

His eight cast members were a bickering but tight-knit family, held together by a shared passion for too much lipstick, glittering feather boas, and Colombian buds. Angel had a budget for sets and costumes, a backstage crew and the free apartment, with views of the historic district and the Port of Tampa.

But today, flat charcoal clouds had settled over Ybor like a shroud. Looking down from his window at 15th Street and the wide sidewalks that lined it, Angel imagined where he might land if he jumped. With his arms and legs akimbo on the concrete, he pictured the chalk mark around his body as a jagged piece from a jigsaw puzzle.

Then he turned back to his room and pulled the damp sheets off the bed.

Josh had told him that night sweats and swollen lymph nodes were early signs of the virus.

Wearing his dad's plaid bathrobe and red wool slippers, he stared into the bathroom mirror - the one installed for a person taller than 5-feet-2. If he stretched up on his tiptoes, and leaned his head back, he could almost see his neck.

His fingers pressed around under his jaw.

Where the hell were your lymph nodes? Was that a swollen lump?

It must be.

Clearly, he was dying.

Just like Rock Hudson and Angel Wilson of the *B-52s* last year.

And just like Liberace, whose death in early February proved that floor-length furs, gold-plated Rolls Royces and all those filigreed arpeggios couldn't protect you from this virus.

And just like his friend Frankie, the most handsome man in Ybor City, not even 30, who went into the hospital the first weekend of January with pneumonia and came out three days later in a body bag.

***

Angel had lived in Ybor a little more than a month when one of the drag queens told him about the full-moon celebration at Frankie and Josh's two-story bungalow on Fifth Avenue. Even though they'd gone to high school together, Angel wasn't sure Frankie knew who he was.

Angel had worked El Goya's Saturday night show and it was 11 when he pushed open the wrought iron gate and stepped into a raucous, dancing crowd packing a walled, red-brick patio that covered half a city block. Before he could take two steps, Frankie pulled Angel into a bear hug.

"I heard you were in Ybor," Frankie said, over the ka-chunk of a dreadlocked reggae band. "I figured I'd run into you sooner or later."

"I didn't think you'd remember me," Angel said.

"Jesuit wasn't that big a place. Of course, I do," said Frankie.

"But I was me and you were Frankie Capitano!"

"I still am," he said, ruffling Angel's hair with his hand.

At Jesuit High in the early 1970s, Angel Torres was an odd flavor in the school's macho stew. Frankie, with his looks and the home run record he set as the Tigers first baseman, was a main ingredient. Angel remembered him wearing a letter sweater and dating winsome brunettes from the Academy of Holy Names.

He never dreamed he and Frankie might be members of the same tribe.

Frankie led him on a tour of the four-bedroom bungalow, with oak floors, a wide front porch and a dining room big enough for an extended Sicilian family. Most Ybor houses were narrow shotgun "casitas", but Frankie's grandfather had started a grocery store that grew into a chain of supermarkets and this had been his home.

Frankie had sunk a hot tub in a back bedroom and replaced the wooden walls with glass that revealed an up-lit garden of orchids and bamboo.

"How about some tub?" Frankie asked.

As Frankie pulled off his white T-shirt and blue jeans, Angel tried not to stare at the tanned rocks that were his shoulders. Frankie looked like a Sicilian Superman, the jaw, the regal nose, even the jet-black ringlet across his forehead.

Next to him, Angel was a little boy who still hadn't grown a single hair on his pale, concave chest. He slipped quickly out of his clothes and into the tub.

"Somehow, I never expected I'd be sitting in a hot tub with you," Angel said.

"Stop it." Frankie laughed. "High school wasn't the real world."

"It felt pretty real to me sometimes," Angel said.

"Yeah. I guess it did."

"I mean, look at me," Angel said. "Everybody knew what I was. My parents knew before I did. But you? Girls? Baseball? I just thought…"

"Baseball was fun. You ever been in a locker room after a game?" Frankie laughed. "Talk about homo-erotic."

"And the girls?" Angel said.

"These were Academy girls, remember? We weren't actually having sex. It was more like wrestling. But sex with a woman can be fun. Sex is sex, man!"

Angel tried to pay attention, but he was distracted by the frothy bubbles that rippled a goatee-sized clump of jet-black hair on Frankie's chest.

"…but with men I felt something else," Frankie was saying. "And then I met Josh and it all made sense. Love. Whatever you want to call it."

"And your parents are okay with … this?"

Frankie was silent for a long beat.

Angel's mom had kept him up-to-date on Frankie's family. His mother was the debutant daughter of cigar factory royalty. His father compounded his dad's grocery store fortune by transforming acres of North Tampa orange groves into walled and gated enclaves. Frankie supervised the drywall crews for Capitano Construction.

"We don't really talk about it," Frankie finally said.

Just then, Josh appeared in the doorway, already stripped down to his tiny white underwear.

"I thought I'd find you here. And with another man," he said with mock anger, but he was smiling.

Josh was no taller than Angel. He was sandy haired, and as pretty as a girl, with a fine nose, long lashes and the slender, muscled body of a dancer.

"Josh," Frankie told him, "you need to get in here and meet my high school buddy, Angel Torres."

***

If there was a childhood disease going around West Tampa, it always found Angel.

 Over the course of six months after his eighth birthday, Angel ran the table – first measles, then chicken pox, and finally, a scary bout with scarlet fever that left his throat blistered and his tiny body covered in a crimson rash.

As a teenager he endured bronchitis and allergies. The first time he kissed a boy, he contracted mononucleosis.

Adulthood didn't help.

In the club, if one of the queens sneezed, Angel got a cold. He took tiny blue pills that kept his stomach from filling up with acid. The skin on his back was always itchy, due to some untreatable fungus.

He had dandruff.

And now this virus. It had to be the night Frankie talked him into joining him at the baths. It was his first and only time. He had felt out of place among all those handsome, muscled men. He was pretty sure he hadn't had sex with Frankie, but there were so many bodies, it all became a blur. And now, Frankie was dead and now Angel had the virus inside him doing its worst. The morning sweats were just a scouting party preparing the way for an army of killers aiming for his immune system.

Why can't I get a break? Angel thought, as he hung his damp sheets on the curtain rods in his windows to dry.

You spend your adolescence branded a pansy, a sissy, a fag. You struggle to survive as the kids you played with in elementary school,

178

like Eddie Valdez, turn on you.

His sophomore year, Angel had caught Eddie scrawling "COCKSUCKER!" on his locker.

"Eddie, what the hell?" Angel had shouted, wishing his voice hadn't risen to a higher register on the last word.

"What's it taste like?" Eddie shouted back, as he stuck the Magic Marker back in his pants pocket.

"What?"

Eddie, a granite boulder of a guy who anchored Jesuit's offensive line, looked around at the teenage boys who had gathered to witness the commotion. He let his voice soften, sounding almost like an old friend.

"All that cum? I mean, does it always taste the same or are there different flavors depending on the cock you're sucking?"

You survive that and all the other humiliations. You make it to college and find a life in the theater and dance department, and some friends, even some actual boyfriends. You play Che Guevara in a much-lauded production of *Evita* and your mom hangs the framed review – illustrated with a picture of you - on her hallway wall.

And just as you start to believe this is your real life, the world hands you a death sentence?

In Dr. Guinta's office last week for his annual check-up, Angel quietly asked for a special blood test. This rotund old Italian, with chalky skin that sagged like a mastiff, had seen him through his childhood maladies. Dr. Guinta nodded solemnly at the request, slipped on plastic gloves, and got out the blood vial.

"Don't tell my mom, okay? I don't want to worry her."

Dr. Guinta tapped the inside of Angel's elbow, then eased a needle into a bulging vein.

Angel wouldn't get the results for several days, but he didn't need to wait.

He knew.

He pulled the thermometer from the medicine cabinet, shook it twice, then slipped the glass tip under his tongue, his hands shaking.

I need some Sinatra to calm me down, Angel thought.

Angel's friends favored Judy Garland or Bette Midler. But Angel loved Sinatra. Sure he was probably a royal asshole in real life, but the guy on records was lost and vulnerable and he always seemed to be searching for himself in the lyrics.

Angel kept his records in a half-dozen orange crates under the tall table that held his prized possessions – a Marantz 2245 receiver and a Technics turntable under a smoked plastic lid. Two JBL speakers, each the size of a dorm-room refrigerator, rested on pedestals against the wall.

With the thermometer tight between his lips, Angel knelt in front of the bin labeled SINATRA and flipped past *Songs for Swinging Lovers*, *Come Fly With Me*, *Songs For Young Lovers*, and *The Capitol Years* boxed set. He kept flipping until he found the album he wanted.

In the Wee Small Hours was Sinatra's elegy to Ava Gardner, the woman he loved and lost. The cover was a watercolor of Sinatra smoking a cigarette as he leaned grimly against a wall on some urban back street, a lone lamppost in the distance.

Sinatra's sadness had a patina of street coolness that Angel craved. His own sadness was always punctuated by embarrassing crying spells, stomach cramps and a runny nose.

Angel wiped the vinyl with his lint-free cloth and set the record gently on the black rubber pad of the turntable. He lifted the cartridge, willing his hands to stop shaking as he set it on the proper track.

There was Sinatra's oaky voice. Cole Porter's bittersweet lyrics.

What is this thing called love?
This funny thing called love?
Who can solve its mystery?
Why should it make a fool of me?

Angel started a slow dance around the room, pulling the thermometer from his mouth. He could feel the first tears on his cheeks. He danced near the window so he could see exactly how far north the blood-red line had climbed in the glass tube.

I saw you there one wonderful day
And you took my heart and threw it away.
Now I ask the Lord in heaven above.
What is this thing called love?

Shit, he thought, squinting at the mercury a second time to make sure he was seeing it correctly.

Ninety-eight-point-six.

How could that be?

***

Josh was in Tampa for just a week, nursing a freshly broken heart, when he met Frankie.

He had never heard a pick-up line during Holy Communion before, but the guy behind him had clearly whispered in his ear, "Bless me father for I'd like to sin."

Josh turned quickly and there was Elvis, at least a guy who looked like the Elvis from the 1950s. When Josh returned to his pew, Elvis slid in next to him. They sat silently for a moment as a soloist sang

Panis Angelicus.

"I thought you might like to join me at a prayer meeting this evening?" Elvis whispered.

"Is it my immortal soul that interests you? Or something else?" Josh whispered back.

"We'll need to pray about that."

Josh didn't really do clever banter. He was a dark thinker who could imagine a storm lurking behind the whitest clouds. It wasn't the best thing for his love life.

On a bitter cold morning in late February, Garrett, the aspiring dancer Josh had met his first week at Julliard, had told him, over ceramic mugs of coffee at a Greek diner, that he was headed to Cancun on spring break with someone else.

"I need a little more sunlight in my life," Garrett said. "And a little less Chopin."

After Garrett's announcement, Josh had fled to Florida hoping to outrun his misery. Instead, he had spent six days diving deep into darkness.

Josh's passions ran toward ballet, opera and Chopin. He had studied dance, but had earned his scholarship to Julliard playing the oboe. He loved funereal dirges, dying swans and unhappy endings. He didn't really blame Garrett, but losing him didn't hurt any less.

After the service, on the steps of Christ the King, under a harshly optimistic March sun, Frankie introduced himself. He told Josh he'd never tried to pick up anyone in church before.

"It's weird. I saw you and I felt like maybe we've met before?" he said.

"Now that's a pick-up line," Josh said.

Standing next to Frankie, Josh felt like he had pulled on a soft leather glove. He wasn't used to that kind of comfort with the men in his life. It scared him.

"I should tell you now that I'm nursing a broken heart," Josh announced. "I'm prone to sudden dark moods and thoughts of death and decay, and I don't listen to any music written after 1880. You've been warned."

Frankie laughed.

"And I'm a recovering athlete who loves Kiss. We all have crosses to bear. So what are you doing at Christ the King?"

"I promised my mom that no matter what else I did, I'd get to mass every week."

"See, you're a good boy. Like me."

"That's what I'm afraid of. My last one was a good boy and now he's making sure to stay about 2,000 miles away from me."

"So I like a challenge. And you like my pick-up lines. How's this: what are you doing later?"

Josh gave in.

"I'm flying back to New York tomorrow, but I've got nothing until then."

"It's beach blanket night at the Tampa baths. It's a lot of fun."

"I'm not really a baths kind of guy," Josh said. "It's too confusing. What did that comedian say – 'I don't go to orgies - too many thank you notes'."

"That's funny. My friend calls the baths 'holy communion for homos.' He may be right. But anyway, we can skip that. How about dinner at my house?"

***

Two days after Frankie died, Josh received a registered letter from the law firm of Angelo Capitano, Frankie's uncle. In precise legal language, the letter explained that Josh was not welcome at the funeral. He had a month to "vacate the Capitano family home."

"We'll plan an Ybor memorial," Angel suggested, after he read the letter. "In the club. We can invite everybody."

They were drinking café con leche at El Goya's corner coffee shop. Angel started to fold up the letter, then changed his mind. He crumpled the paper in his fist.

"You don't mind, do you?"

Josh shook his head.

"So are you okay?" Angel asked.

"I'm positive, if that's what you're asking. But I'm not sick and my T-cell count is good. I just can't sleep or eat. I started crying last night watching an ATT commercial about a guy calling his family back home."

"What are you gonna do now? We could find you an apartment in Ybor."

"Ybor was Frankie. So now Ybor's over. I'm going back to Long Island for a while. Maybe back to school. See what happens."

Angel wanted to be comforting, but he had so many questions.

"Had Frankie been sick? I mean, it happened so fast."

"We'd wake up some mornings and the sheets were wet. Night sweats, they called it. And the lymph nodes, around his neck, they were swollen. But that was it. I had told him to get tested. But he never got there. The pneumonia seemed to come out of nowhere."

Angel nodded. He wasn't sure Josh knew about the night he and Frankie visited the baths. He wasn't about to mention it now.

"I've got an idea for the memorial," Angel said, eager to change the subject. "I was thinking we could restage *Kiss My Asp*. We can take that picture of Frankie in the costume and blow it up."

It had been Angel's idea to restage the terrible '60s epic, Cleopatra, as a drag show called Kiss My Asp. Frankie had made a cameo appearance.

Josh laughed at the suggestions, then leaned over, taking Angel's head in his hands and, pulling him closer, planted a kiss on his forehead.

"I'd love that. He would too," he said, his face close to Angel's.

"I'm not really a show biz guy," Frankie had said when Angel called. "I don't sing. I don't dance. You need Josh. He's the dancer in our family."

"What I have in mind is a role only you can play. It's what we call a walk-on."

A week later, Frankie "walked on" from a balsa wood and cardboard barge dressed in a very skimpy toga, his biceps wrapped in tight gold bands, his tree-trunk legs in calf-high golden sandals, a crown of lilac leaves pressed into jet black curls.

He literally stopped the show.

"Hail yes, Caesar!" Maria von Tramp shouted.

She and the other cast members were dressed as Cleopatra's courtiers. They all swooned at Caesar's sandaled feet.

When the audience settled down, Helga Heine, a drag queen even taller and more muscled than Frankie, emerged as a very butch Cleopatra.

"Ides of March my ass," Helga quipped, as she ran her hands over Frankie's chest. "I say beware of Caesar. After rehearsal last night I grabbed this Italian stallion's mighty sword and let me tell you girls he ripped me from limb to limb. By the end, I'm beating on his chest – '*et tu, you big brute*! *ET TU!!!!*' If not for all the Playtex holding my lady parts together, Cleo wouldn't be standing up here tonight."

The crowd was back on its feet whooping and applauding. From the light booth, Angel could see Frankie blushing through his make-up.

"Frankie said he hated it, but he really loved all the attention," Josh told Angel. "Just one request. I have to play Cleopatra. You think Helga will mind?" Josh asked.

"I'll take care of Helga. What's your idea?"

"I'm not sure yet, but that Sunday at the hospital, he came around for about five minutes. His family had gone down to the coffee shop and I was able to slip into the room. They hadn't let me see him. But I sat outside his room for three days and nights. When I whispered his name, his eyes opened. And he was just so calm. It was like he came back from somewhere to tell me something."

"To tell you what?"

"He made me promise I'd dance at his funeral."

Angel nodded. He loved this plan.

But after Josh left the restaurant, Angel felt something like a knife twisting deep inside his groin. If Frankie could die of this new virus, Angel couldn't be far behind.

The next morning, he woke to his first set of soaked bed sheets.

***

For the finale of the memorial service two weeks later, eight drag queens in polyester togas and sheer chiffon gowns carried Cleopatra onstage atop a golden litter.

Angel cued the music – slow, sensuous drums, the soft strumming of an *oud*, the Arabic lute, and a mournful violin line that seemed to float above and below the rhythm.

Josh made a beautiful Egyptian queen, in a cream-colored sleeveless gown wrapped with a gold lame belt, and trimmed in sequins and metallic braiding. His black, shoulder-length wig was topped with a headpiece glittering with faux blue gems on a triangle over his forehead.

Stepping off the litter, Cleopatra set a straw, snake-charmer's basket at center stage.

Angel's cast stood solemnly in a half-circle, watching as the Queen of the Nile danced slowly around the basket.

She moved to the easel where the photo of Frankie as Caesar was blown up and mounted on poster board. Cleopatra's bejeweled hand slid from Frankie's face to his feet.

She stretched up and kissed the image of Frankie's lips, then belly danced slowly back to the basket.

At this point, it didn't matter that the coiled snake rising from the basket was foam or that Josh was a small man dressed in Egyptian drag.

In Cleopatra's hands, the snake came to life. She lifted the undulating creature over her head, as she began to spin, quickly at first, then slower and slower.

She brought the snake down in a series of spasmodic jerks, then drew the snake's wide head to her neck and let it linger there, like a lover.

Suddenly, the snake struck, and Cleopatra, recoiling, tossed it to the stage.

Following Josh's instructions, Angel stopped the music.

Lit by a single spot, Cleopatra crumpled slowly to the stage to the sound of gasps and choked-back sobs from the darkened room.

The light held Cleopatra's death scene for a moment, then faded slowly to black.

***

The white winter sunlight pouring through Angel's bare window roused him before seven. At the party after Frankie's memorial the previous night, he had swallowed too much Prosecco and danced until three.

His head throbbed. Angel pressed his eyes shut, hoping the pain, now merging with his usual morning dread, would subside. He couldn't stop his hands from investigating the status of his bedsheets.

They were dry.

Angel pulled up the knitted afgan and let himself fall back into sleep. In his dream, he was six years old and riding his bike on a path under the oak trees of MacFarland Park in West Tampa. His cousin raced ahead of him and Angel pumped his pedals hard to catch up.

The ringing phone snapped him back.

"Did I call too early?"

"It's okay, Mom. I'm being lazy today. What's up?"

"I saw Dr. Guinta at Publix yesterday. He said his nurse tried to call you but nobody answered."

Angel sat up. He felt the familiar fire kindling in his belly.

"My machine hasn't been picking up, I guess."

"He says you're dehydrated. Remember what I told you about drinking more water?"

"What else did he say?"

"He said he's thinking about retiring. Letting that woman doctor - what's her name? - take over his practice. Me, I don't like women doctors. I'm sure they know what they're doing, but I just don't like it."

"Did he say anything else about me?"

"He said to call him if you need anything, but otherwise, he'll see you next year. Or maybe she'll see you next year."

After they said goodbye, Angel climbed out of bed, pulling the afgan around him like a Joseph's coat, and went to his window.

Florida cold fronts are Janus-faced. The first day, Gothic clouds crush your spirit, icy slivers of rain pierce any inflated hopes. If the clouds and rain linger for two days, weaker souls can find themselves leaning out of third-story windows contemplating the sidewalk below.

But overnight the clouds clear and the sun rises from the bay, shiny as a pirate's doubloon. The air is crisp, the sky high and cloudless.

A day like this can be deceiving, Angel thought. Frankie was still dead. Lots of others, too.

But looking out on the brick battlements of old Ybor and the shimmering blue of Tampa Bay in the distance, Angel realized that, for this one moment, he was almost happy.

ABOUT THE AUTHOR

As a journalist, Paul Wilborn collected multiple awards from the American Society of Newspaper Editors and the Florida Society of Newspaper Editors. He won the Green Eyeshade Award from the Atlanta Chapter of Sigma Delta Chi, the South's top writing prize. Based on a selection of his writing, Wilborn was chosen for the Paul Hansel Award, Florida's top journalism prize. He was a Knight-Wallace Fellow at the University of Michigan.

His plays have been produced at Stageworks, Off-Center Theater, Radio Theater Project, and University of Michigan.

He was a founding member of Ybor City's Artists and Writers Group.

Cigar City is his debut short story collection. He is currently at work on two novels set in Florida, Trickle Down and Moonlight Bay.

Wilborn is executive director of the Palladium Theater at St. Petersburg College and lives in Saint Petersburg with his wife, the film actor Eugenie Bondurant.

Made in the USA
Middletown, DE
05 May 2019